ENCOUNTER
AT COLD
HARBOR

Bonnets and Bugles Series   8

ENCOUNTER AT COLD HARBOR

GILBERT MORRIS

MOODY PRESS
CHICAGO

ISBN: 0-8024-0918-0

1 3 5 7 9 10 8 6 4 2

Printed in the United States of America

To Troy and Jason Freemon
Hang in there, you guys!
You're the kind of young fellows
I am proud to see growing up in this country!

Contents

1
Jeff Makes a Decision

A pale yellow sun looked down on the streets of Richmond as Jeff Majors made his way along the line of shops. From time to time he saw his reflection in a plate glass window. What he saw was a tall young man wearing an ash-gray uniform with a shock of black hair coming out from beneath his cap. At seventeen he looked older. He already had shoulders broader than most of the men in his company, and there was a sureness about his movements.

After passing several shops, he turned into one and greeted the short, fat storekeeper with a quick nod.

"Howdy, Mr. Bennett!"

"Why, hello, Jeff!" Mr. Bennett was quick to wait on him, for there was only one other customer in the store, a man with one arm missing, who stood looking sadly at the empty shelves that composed most of the store. "What can I do for you today?"

Casting his eyes around the depleted shop, Jeff said, "Not much, it looks like, Mr. Bennett. You're about out of stock."

"Well, in that you're right." The storekeeper nodded glumly. He dropped his head, stared at the floor, then shrugged his bulky shoulders. "If some of them blockade runners don't make it through pretty soon, I'm gonna have to close up."

Jeff was well aware of the shortage of goods in wartime Richmond. Ever since the War Between the States had started, the Federals had thrown a blockade of naval vessels around the coast of the South. It had grown steadily stronger until now only the boldest captains would risk their vessels, for if they were captured they would lose everything they had.

"I guess it's pretty tough, but we'll make it!" Jeff's eyes continued to run around the shelves as he said, "I need some butter. Looks like you got some of that."

"Sure have." Bennett picked up a yellow mound of butter that had been carefully molded. "Woman that keeps cows on the outside of town, she brought this in just this morning. Real fresh."

"How much?" Jeff asked.

"Well, I'll have to get fifteen dollars for it."

Jeff stared at the man. *"Fifteen dollars* for a pound of butter? Why, that's outlandish!"

Bennett licked his lips, then shrugged. "I know it is, and if Confederate money keeps on losing its value, by this time next week it'll be thirty dollars. Better stock up while you can, Jeff!"

Taking the shopkeeper at his word, he collected a few supplies. As Mr. Bennett put them in a box, Jeff pulled a thick fold of bank notes from his pocket. Peeling off several, he said, "Used to be you had to bring your money in your pocket and take your groceries off in a box. If things don't get better, it looks like I'll have to bring the money in a box and take the groceries home in my pocket."

Mr. Bennett took the cash and managed a smile. "Won't be long before we'll whip the Yankees. Then things will get back to normal again." He stared at the money dolefully, then put it into a cigar box beneath the counter. "Tell your pa I said hello!"

"I'll do that, Mr. Bennett!"

Jeff left the store and continued down the street. There was a mournful air about the streets of Richmond that had not been apparent when he and his family had first arrived here from Kentucky. Then, war fever had been at its height. Bands had been playing, and pretty girls had been handing out cookies and glasses of lemonade to farm boys as they flooded into Richmond to fight the Yankees.

As Jeff crossed the dusty street, his mind went back to his old home in Kentucky. *Wish I was back there!* he thought, then shook his shoulders and pushed the thought away. "Can't be thinking about things like that," he murmured aloud. Still, thoughts kept coming to him, mostly thoughts about his boyhood when he and Leah Carter had roamed the hills, fishing, hunting, and looking for birds' eggs. "Sure do miss Leah," Jeff muttered. Then, when he saw a man looking at him strangely, he grinned and said, "Just talkin' to myself!" and laughed as the man smiled.

Many of the men on the street hobbled along on crutches, missing a leg. Many had only one arm. Some had patches over one eye, and their faces were scarred. It was a depressing sight, and Jeff had never gotten used to it.

A large black-and-tan hound thumped his tail against the floor of the post office as Jeff stepped toward the door. Leaning over, he patted its head. "Wish me and you could go out and hunt coon, boy."

The tail thumped again, and Jeff pulled the dog's long ears.

Inside the post office, he waited his turn, studying the notices posted on the walls. The mail did not get priority in the Confederacy, and sometimes it took weeks for a letter to get to its destination. However, when Jeff got to the window and said, "Any mail for Nelson Majors or his family?" he was pleased to see the postmaster nod.

"Yep, got one right here! Just come in!" He handed Jeff a letter and twisted his head to one side and winked. "From your sweetheart, I'll bet!"

Jeff looked at the envelope and saw that it was Leah's handwriting. "That's right!" he said. "Prettiest sweetheart in the whole Confederacy!"

As he turned away, the thought came to him that actually Leah was not *in* the Confederacy. Kentucky had not come out to fight for the South. It was for that reason the Majors family had left there to come to Richmond, where Jeff's mother died shortly after their arrival.

He moved to one side of the walk and leaned against a hardware shop. Across the street, a blacksmith was making a rhythmic clanging as he hammered out a white-hot piece of steel. He heard the hum of voices as people passed and the sound of horses' hooves as men rode by or drove past in wagons and buggies of every sort.

Jeff opened the letter and eagerly read it:

Dear Jeff and all,

I trust that this finds you well. It seems so far away from the war here in Kentucky. The woods are quiet, and there are no sounds of guns, and even Pineville doesn't seem touched by the terrible struggles going on where you are. However, I must be more cheerful. Esther is fine. She is the prettiest, happiest little girl in the whole world! She would love you, and you would love her!

She babbles like a magpie. She is so pretty. She has the same blonde hair and blue eyes your mother had. I think she's going to look just like her when she grows up.

I'm worried about your brother. Tom's discouraged again. For a while he was doing better, but he's much quieter than he used to be. He was always so happy and laughed all the time, but now he hardly says anything. He helps Ezra and my father with the work around the farm, but he goes off by himself for long times.

Ezra made him a fine, wooden leg, as I told you the last time. We finally got him to put it on, and though he limps some, it works fine . . .

Jeff looked up as a drover passed with a wagon full of goods. The man yelled and cracked his whip over the heads of the oxen, which were straining to pull the heavy load. Jeff watched for a moment.

Tom and Sarah, Leah's sister, had planned to get married, but the war had driven them apart. Leah's brother, Royal, was in the Union Army. Tom had served with his father and Jeff in the Army of Northern Virginia until he lost a leg at Gettysburg.

Jeff looked down and read the rest of the letter, devouring the news of the farm and all the things that were going on back home. Finally he sighed, folded the letter, and stuck it into his inside pocket.

He walked on through town and out to the camp just south of Richmond. The sound of bugles, and men drilling, and the many other noises that go with an army camp came to him, but he was so accustomed to them he hardly noticed.

When he got to where his company was sta-

13

tioned, he glanced up at the flag that indicated the officers' headquarters.

The corporal on guard outside the tent winked at him. "Hello, Private Majors! You want to see your pa—I mean Colonel Majors?"

"If he's not busy."

"Just go right on in! He said he's been looking for you."

Jeff found his father, Col. Nelson Majors, sitting at a portable desk and staring at a map that was laid out before him. Jeff thought again how fine his father looked. He was a dark-skinned man with hazel eyes and a black mustache. At the age of forty-one, he had hair that was still totally black. Looking up, he grinned. "Hello, Jeff. Did you get something to eat?"

"Yes, I did, Pa—I mean Colonel. It cost the world, though!" He put down the box and exhibited his purchases. Then he handed over the remains of the cash and said, "It was the best I could do. The store's about out of everything."

Colonel Majors leaned back and took a deep breath. Balancing himself on the back two legs of his camp chair, he put his hands behind his head and stared up at the tent roof. "Well," he said thoughtfully, "it's not good—but it's better than what we'll get when we take to the field."

At that moment, a tall, rangy captain walked through the door and saluted.

The colonel returned the salute and said, "Well, Captain Dawes, how do the new recruits look?"

Dawes lounged at ease in front of the desk and shrugged his shoulders. "Not like much, Colonel. I guess all the good ones have already been scooped up. Some of them we got in this bunch are either

14

too old to do much good or so young I hate to see them coming on."

Jeff said instantly, "I'm as old as some of them, Pa—Colonel."

"Now don't you start on me, Jeff! You're not joining the Regulars! You're going to be a drummer boy at least a few more months. Let's hear no more of it!" Colonel Majors looked down at his map. "Not much question about what's going to happen next, is there, Captain?"

Dawes bit his lower lip. "Reckon not, sir. I hear Grant's got an army of a hundred thousand men ready to feed into this here war. I wish we had half that many!"

"Then we'll just have to do better. Every man will have to cover a little more ground and fight a little harder. We knew all this would happen when the war started."

Then the two men talked about the battle that was to come.

Throughout the early years of the war, the South had won battle after battle, but the superior weight and the manufacturing power of the North were now ready to roll. Every time a Southern soldier fell, he left a gap in the ranks. When a Northern boy was taken, all General Grant had to do was reach into the city and pick up a recruit. Many in the North were tired of the war, but President Lincoln was now sure he had found a fighting general.

"I've heard about Grant," Colonel Majors said. "They say he's merciless!"

"Yes, sir, and now that we've lost Stonewall Jackson, it's going to be harder. After Gettysburg, we're down mighty thin! Where do you think they'll hit?"

"Right up in this area, and we'll be moving out soon, Captain Dawes, so get these men trained as quick as you can! That's all!"

"Yes, sir!"

Colonel Majors waited until the captain had left the tent, then said, "It's going to be mighty tough, Jeff."

"We can whip 'em, sir!"

A smile flashed across Colonel Majors's lips, then he said slowly, "You know what I've been thinking about? Kentucky."

"Oh, and I just got a letter from Leah. Wait'll you hear what she says about Esther!" Jeff handed the letter to his father and waited until he had finished reading. "She sounds like a beauty, doesn't she? Says she looks just like Ma!"

A frown creased the colonel's brow, and his lips drew down tightly. He moved uneasily in his chair, then finally got up and walked to the tent flap. He stared out for such a long time that Jeff wondered what he could be thinking.

Finally his father turned back and said, "Jeff, I think so much about Esther—and about your mother."

"Well, I do too, and I know Tom does."

"I don't feel right about letting the Carters do all the raising of my daughter. It just seems like I've let your mother down somehow."

"But you couldn't help it, Pa!"

After Mrs. Majors's death, it had been the Carters back in Kentucky who volunteered to raise baby Esther until such time as the Majors men could get settled. That meant, of course, when the war was over, but being separated from the child had been hard on all of them.

16

"Maybe after this next battle the Yankees'll quit and go home. Then the war will be over, and we can get her back again."

Jeff's words did not seem to reach Colonel Majors. He returned to his chair and said thoughtfully, "It's hard not being able to have your child. I think about it all the time. I wish there was some way that we could take her, but I guess there's not."

Uncomfortable, Jeff moved toward the tent door. He did not like to see his father so downcast.

After bidding the colonel good-bye, he went to his own unit, where he was surrounded by his squad and took part in the activities that went on, including cooking supper. But after eating, he sat by himself for a long time in the tent that he shared with the other young men. Finally he clamped his jaw and said, "There's *got* to be a way! Lord, please show me what to do!"

He waited for a moment as if he expected the Lord to speak out of heaven. Then he laughed aloud at himself. "Well, I *know* what I'm going to do! I'm going to write Leah!"

He found a scrap of paper that had already been used for a letter, crossed out the used side, and then with a stub of pencil began to write:

Dear Leah,
    There's something I want you to think about. You see, my pa and I miss Esther an awful lot . . .

2

Tom Makes a Decision

The lanky, blue-nosed mule that stopped in front of the Dan Carter home was straddled by an equally lanky rider. Pete Mangus pulled back on the leather reins, saying, "Whoa, Clementine, hang on there just a minute, will ya!"

Leah Carter emerged from the white frame house to see Pete peer past the picket fence and touch his hat with his left hand. "Well, howdy there, Miss Leah!"

"Hello, Pete!" At sixteen Leah had grown out of the gawky stage. She still saw herself, however, as a tall, awkward girl, though her mother had told her many times, "You're going to be a beautiful woman. Don't mind it—just think about how awkward the colts look until they get their full growth." Leah's eyes were sea green, and she allowed her long blonde hair to fall down the back of the simple blue-and-white dress that reached almost to her ankles.

Pete Mangus kept his eyes fixed on her with evident pleasure. "Wal," he said casually, shifting his weight on Clementine's back, "don't you look pretty now!" At that moment he spotted a huge grasshopper crawling along the ground and expertly loosed an amber stream of tobacco juice that drowned the insect. Pete nodded, satisfied with his aim, and then turned back to Leah. "You expectin' a letter, are ya, Leah?"

Leah knew that he loved to tease her about her letters from Jeff. She was accustomed to this and said eagerly, "Yes, and I bet you got one from Jeff, haven't you?"

"Well, that might be." Pete fumbled through the letter sack that hung beside his leg, finally coming up with an envelope. He peered at it as if he had never seen it before. "Well, dog my cats, sure enough!" He held the letter close to his eyes, and his lips moved as he read the words. "'Miss Leah Carter, Pineville, Kentucky.' Yep, I reckon it's for you, all right!" He looked down and saw Leah reach for it but did not hand it to her at once. "I expect you and that young man are gettin' mighty serious, Leah."

"Oh, Pete, give me the letter! Please!"

Pete, however, held onto it. "That sister of yours and that young Rebel, they ain't aimin' to marry up, are they?"

This was a question that came up often. Tom Majors had been brought back to Pineville to recuperate after losing his leg. He and Sarah Carter had been practically engaged when the war broke out, and many were speculating on whether or not Sarah would have him now.

Pete said, "I expect she didn't calculate on no one-legged man. That might change things, don't you think, Leah?"

Knowing Pete could be the most terrible gossip in Kentucky, Leah refused to get into a discussion. "I don't know, Pete. That's their business. Now, let me have the letter, please!" She took the envelope as he reluctantly extended it, and began to walk away.

Pete called out after her, "I'd be glad to hear what Jeff has to say, Leah." When she paid him no attention, he kicked his heels against the mule and sighed. "Come on, Clementine, we can't stand here all day! We got the mail to deliver!"

Leah considered going to her own room to read the letter, but news was so precious that she thought it was only fair to share with the family. Her parents, Sarah, Morena, and Tom were seated around the table when she entered the dining room and held up the letter. "It's from Jeff!"

Tom Majors, sitting across the table from Sarah, looked up quickly. He was a tall young man, dark complected but still pale from the ordeal of losing his leg. He had the same dark hair and hazel eyes as his father and had a rather sad look about him. "What does he say, Leah? Are they all right?"

"I haven't read it yet. I thought you'd all want to hear it." Leah opened the letter.

They watched as she scanned the letter. Her father, Dan, was a thin, sickly looking man. Her mother, who had the same blonde hair and green eyes that one saw in Leah, was holding three-year-old Esther on her lap. Sarah had dark hair, dark blue eyes, and a beautiful complexion. From time to time her eyes went across to Tom. Leah's sister Morena sat next to Sarah. Morena was a beautiful young girl—but one who had never developed mentally. She could do simple things such as dress herself, but she never spoke and was like a small child in her mind.

"Well, what does he say?" Sarah asked. "Is he all right? Is Colonel Majors all right?"

"Yes," Leah said slowly, "but it's not what I thought." Looking around the table, she saw their anxiety and added quickly, "Oh, they're both all right. Neither one of them has been wounded or

20

anything like that, but Jeff says his father's got a problem."

"Well, can you read it to us, or is it too private?" her father asked.

Leah hesitated, then said, "March the twentieth is when it was written. I'll read it out loud." She began:

Dear Leah,
    There's something I want you to think about. You see, my pa and I miss Esther an awful lot. Pa is awful down in the mouth, Leah. You know how he's always been real happy and able to handle anything, but he's worried now and it's about Esther. What it is, he thinks he's letting Ma down by not having a hand in her raising. He thinks he ought to be doing more, and nothing I say makes him feel any better . . .

The letter went on about how bad Nelson Majors felt being separated from his daughter.

Finally Tom said abruptly, "I know he's always felt bad. All of us feel bad about it!" Then he seemed to think about how that sounded, and he quickly glanced at Mr. and Mrs. Carter. "Not that we aren't grateful for all you've done. Nobody could've done more, but—"

"I know how it is," Dan Carter said sympathetically. "A man wants to have his children around him. I know how I'd feel if one of my young ones was growing up and I couldn't have nothin' to do with 'em."

"That's exactly right!" Mrs. Carter said. She shifted Esther around to where she could look into the child's face and smiled gently, touching the rosy

21

cheek with a forefinger. "And Esther needs to see her pa, too. Why, I bet she'd know him in no time!"

"Well," Leah said, "that's exactly what Jeff says." She continued reading:

> What I want to ask you to do, Leah, is to help me pray for some way to bring Esther to Richmond. There's no chance at all that Pa or me can get back to Kentucky. I know there's going to be another big battle soon, and I know it sounds impossible, but your pa always said that with God all things are possible. That was his favorite verse, I reckon. And now I'm asking for you to pray that somehow you can get Esther back here.
>
> Well, that's all for right now. I miss you and look forward to the time when I'll see you again.
>
> Your friend,
> Jeff Majors

A moment of silence ran around the table, and Mrs. Carter reached over and stroked Morena's hair. Then she said, "I'll help you pray for that, Leah. I know Colonel Majors needs to see his little girl."

A frown crossed her father's face. "Well, there ain't no doubt that it would be a good thing, but I don't see how in the world it could happen! With a war going on, just *gettin'* to Richmond would be a chore. And to get a small child down there? Why, the trains ain't runnin' most of the time, and some of 'em not at all! I just don't hardly see how it could be done."

"But with God all things *are* possible," Leah said. "That's what you always said, Pa."

Grinning, Dan Carter smoothed his thinning hair. "Well, if you're gonna start throwin' Scripture back at me, I ain't got no answer for that. I guess we'll all just have to pray for it."

"*I* could take her to Richmond," Leah said abruptly.

"All by yourself? Don't be foolish, child!" Her mother shook her head sharply. "It would be no trip for a young girl like you to take!"

"Ma, I'm almost grown!"

"*I* could take her," Sarah said, glancing at Tom.

"No, you couldn't!" he said. "Remember how you were warned to stay out of Richmond after they accused you of being a spy?"

Sarah sniffed. "Why, they've forgotten all about that! It was all made up by that Confederate officer anyhow!"

"No, I reckon Tom's right, Sarah," her father said. "It wouldn't do for you to go back." He toyed with his fork, making a design on the tablecloth. "We'll all just have to pray that God will open up a way."

For the next few days, Dan Carter found himself the target of many pleas from Leah, which he steadfastly refused. She insisted she was old enough and mature enough to make the trip. He insisted that it would be too dangerous for her.

"It would be dangerous for Esther too!" he said, as Leah for the tenth time asked for his permission. The two were sitting on the front porch as the sun went down. They had been admiring the sky's red glow tinged with pink and orchid tones, and now the sun, a big yellow globe, seemed to be sinking into the side of the mountains to the west.

Leah had used every argument she had. In desperation she said finally, "But, Pa, think about if it was you and you hadn't seen me or Sarah or Morena. Wouldn't you want Colonel Majors to send us to you if things were turned around that way?"

"Of course, I would! But . . ." Her father teetered on the back two legs of his chair and whittled slowly on the long piece of red cedar in his hands. The razor edge of the knife sliced off a thin, curling piece of the fragrant wood, and it fell onto a small pile that lay at his feet. Looking up at Leah, he added, "I'd do it myself in a minute, but I'm not able to go. I wish I was. And your ma can't go. There just ain't no way—unless God does it Himself."

This was all Leah could get out of her father, and she reluctantly determined not to say anything more to him about it.

Sarah thought Tom grew even more withdrawn after the news came that his father wanted Esther in Richmond. She watched him hobble around on his wooden leg, never complaining, although she knew it pained him at times.

She figured he knew he'd behaved abominably about the leg. He'd sat around the farm for weeks, refusing to even speak, and would not listen to anything about an artificial leg. Only Ezra Payne's persistence, along with hers and Leah's, had persuaded him. Then he kept to himself, thinking dark thoughts, even after mastering use of the wooden limb.

Sarah found him out beside the fence, watching the newest litter of pigs as they grunted at their mother's side. It was hot, and she wore a cool dress made of cotton, which outlined her trim figure. Her

24

black hair caught the last rays of the red sun as it went behind the mountains. Stepping up beside Tom, she looked at the pigs. "You wouldn't think pigs could be cute, would you?"

"I guess anything's cute when it's little—even a pig."

The two stood talking for some time about unimportant things, then turned to go back to the house. When they were halfway there, Sarah caught his arm and pulled him around. "Tom," she said with a question in her voice and in her eyes, "what's going to happen to us?"

"Happen to us? I reckon it's already happened," Tom said, and there was bitterness in his tone. "I don't reckon that we've got any future, Sarah."

"Because you lost a leg? I thought we had all this settled. A man's more than a leg."

"It's all right for you to say that, but I'm the one who has to make the livin'. How can a one-legged man care for a wife and a family?"

"Why, Tom Majors, I reckon you can do just about anything you set your mind to!"

Tom stared at her briefly, stirred for the moment, it seemed, by her words. "I used to think that too, Sarah, but think how hard it'd be to be a farmer. I've tried to plow, and I just can't keep up with Ezra."

"There's more to farming than *plowing*. You can always hire a hand to do that!" Sarah said steadfastly. "I just thank God every day that it wasn't worse. You could've been killed!"

"Sometimes I wish I had been."

"Tom, don't talk like that!" Sarah put her hand on his chest, then laid it on his cheek. Her touch was soft as a feather.

25

Reaching up, he placed a hand over hers and held it. Finally he said in despair, "I'd like it if things were like they used to be, but they never will be, Sarah!"

"I thought you wanted to *marry* me!"

"That was when I was a whole man!"

"We've talked about this! You *are* a whole man! A man is what he is in his heart and in his mind!"

Tom stood there, perhaps trying to believe her words, but finally the depression that had been eating at him for some time seemed to overpower him. Heavily he said, "I've made up my mind. I'd never let you tie yourself to a cripple, Sarah."

He pulled away, and she watched him limp down the path toward the house. Tears rose to her eyes, and she almost called after him. But she realized that the Tom Majors she had known might have lost a leg but he had retained all the Majors stubbornness. Slowly she followed him to the house and went inside.

Leah was sitting at the table with her father, studying arithmetic. Dan Carter had a fine grasp of the subject, and Leah was very poor at it. She could not keep her mind on numbers today, and from time to time she lifted her eyes to the homemade calendar that hung on the wall. She had made it herself, and every day she checked off the day before she went to bed. She got up to cross out April first. "I forgot to do that last night. Yesterday was April Fools' Day, and you forgot it!"

"I reckon I did," her father said. He looked down at the figures and began explaining them again, but at that moment Tom came in. "Well, hello, Tom! You been out walkin' again?"

Tom stood by Dan Carter's chair. "I been thinkin' a lot, Mr. Carter," he said. He sat down slowly and clasped his hands in front of him. "I think you're right about Leah. She's too young to go on that trip by herself."

"I am not!" Leah protested.

"Yes, you are, daughter! Now, hush!" Dan Carter turned back to Tom. "Have you thought of something else?"

"Well, I should've thought of it first off." Tom moved in his chair and then straightened his back. "*I'll* take Esther to Richmond. It's time I was leaving here anyhow."

Dan Carter stared at his young friend. "Are you sure you could make it? Your leg's going to be all right?"

"I'll be all right!" Tom said shortly. He never liked anyone to refer to his injury. "It's time for me to go back. I need to get back where I belong."

"But you can't go in the army!" Leah said, then wished she had not. "I mean—"

"I know. I can't march with one leg, but maybe Pa can find something for me to do. Maybe be a clerk in headquarters." Bitterness came to his lips then, and he said, "I can't do much, but I'll do what I can."

Leah walked over and stood beside Tom. She put her hand on his shoulder, looking down at him, thinking how much he looked like Jeff. "Then, if you go, I'm going with you. You couldn't take care of a three-year-old!"

Tom looked up and found a smile. "Why—that would be good, if it's all right with your Pa."

"Well, of course it's all right with *you* along, Tom! Wouldn't be good to ship the poor child off with just a man to take care of her. She needs a woman!"

Leah smiled brilliantly. "I can do it, Pa! I'm going to tell Ma right now!"

As soon as the girl left the room, Tom shook his head. "It still could be dangerous, Mr. Carter. You know what it's like in wartime."

"I won't worry about it a minute with you there, Tom. You Majorses have a way of doin' what you set out to do." He rose and slapped the young man on the shoulder. "I'm mighty glad you decided to do this. Your pa will be glad to see you, too—although we'll miss you around here."

"I'll miss you too, sir."

From that moment on, the house was in a flurry as everyone got things ready for the journey to Richmond.

The Carter family stood waiting for the stage-coach to arrive. The stage would take Leah and Tom and Esther to the train in Lexington, and from there they would travel by rail to Richmond. Because so many of the railroads were out, the trip would take a long time.

Sarah was sure Leah wasn't thinking about that. Her sister was eagerly standing beside Tom, holding Esther in her arms, when the coach pulled up.

Sarah and her father and mother and Morena each gave Leah a quick kiss. Her parents and Morena all shook hands with Tom.

When it was Sarah's turn to say good-bye to him, she looked up, expecting him to kiss her.

Instead, he awkwardly extended his hand. "Good-bye, Sarah," he said gruffly. He got into the coach with Leah and Esther, the driver cracked his whip, and the coach pulled out.

Sarah stood watching them go, and sadness came over her. *He didn't even kiss me good-bye,* she thought. She watched until the stagecoach disappeared in a cloud of dust down the road, then turned to go with her family back to the house. She knew it would be an empty house for her, but there was no other way.

3
Back in Richmond

Leah dabbed the edge of her handkerchief in the cup of water that Tom brought her and ineffectively wiped Esther's face. The passenger car swayed from side to side, almost violently. She had to hold tightly to the child to keep her from falling off her lap.

"There," she said finally, "that's the best I can do."

"Here," Tom said, "let me hold her a while, Leah." He took Esther and seated himself on the hard, horsehide seat next to Leah. Studying the child, he grinned, saying, "I believe she's a better traveler than either one of us. She even seems to like it."

As they had suspected, the railway systems were so disrupted by the war that they had to change trains innumerable times. However, Esther had made the trip well all the way from Kentucky. She had even flourished on the journey. Right now she struggled to get down to the floor, but Tom held her tightly.

"No, you can't get down," he said. "Here, stand up beside me and look out the window." He turned her toward the glass.

This seemed to please Esther well. As the landscape flashed by, she chattered almost constantly.

"It's been a long trip," Tom said. "I know you're worn out, Leah."

"I'll be glad to lie down on a bed again." Leah groaned, straightening her back painfully. "It's hard to sleep sitting up in one of these seats."

"Sure is!" Tom looked out the window and said abruptly, "Looks like we're pulling into Richmond. There's the siding right over there."

"Won't be too soon for me!" Leah brightened and brushed away some cinders that had come in through the open window. Her face was smeared with smut. "We look like we've come from a sideshow!"

"I guess it beats walking." Tom held onto Esther tightly. "Pa will sure be glad to see Esther again."

"He'll be glad to see you too, Tom."

Tom did not answer for a while, and when he did he changed the subject. Turning to Leah, he said, "I guess you'll be glad to see Jeff."

"I guess so."

"You *guess* so!" Tom jeered. "You two are thick as thieves. Always have been!"

They talked about the time Leah and Jeff had gotten lost in the woods and Tom had to go find them. "You two always were close," he said, holding tightly to Esther as the train clanked and rattled over the rails, swaying from side to side. "Must be nice to have a built-in sweetheart. You don't have to make any decisions."

"Oh, don't be foolish, Tom!"

"Nothing foolish about that!" He watched the tall buildings as the train rolled into the outskirts of Richmond. "Most girls have an awful time courting, have all kinds of fellows, and can't make up their minds."

He'd always liked to tease Leah, and now, she thought, he seemed to be light of spirit for a change.

31

"But you and Jeff—why, you just grew up together."

Leah was watching the buildings of Richmond also. Finally she said quietly, "That's just the trouble, Tom."

"What trouble?"

"Jeff never thinks about me as a woman. He thinks about me as a little girl." She touched her hair and, feeling the grittiness of it, made a face. "I guess he'll always think of me as just the little girl he went hunting birds' eggs with."

Tom studied her. "Well, you look a lot better than you did when you were eleven or twelve. You were all legs and arms then and gawky as a crane." He laughed. "I think you used to cry about that every day!"

"I did!" Leah admitted. "I thought I was too tall, and I still think so!"

"You're not too tall for Jeff. He's going to be taller than either Pa or me. Why, he might be six one or two by the time he stops growing."

"It won't make any difference," she said. She sat quietly for so long that Tom must have noticed she was worried.

"What's wrong, Leah? I thought you'd be glad to get back to see Jeff and Uncle Silas."

Leah thought, then said, "It's hard to grow up, Tom. I sometimes don't know whether I'm a girl or a woman. I'm just halfway in between."

Tom reached over and patted her on the shoulder. "Well, believe it or not, it's hard for boys to grow up too. Hard to know when to act like a man and when to act like a baby." He smiled. "I heard a funny story about Lincoln. Somebody asked him how he took a loss, and he said, 'Well, when I was a boy, things would happen and I would cry.' He said, 'Now I'm too old to cry, and it hurts too much to laugh.'"

Leah could not help smiling too. "I guess that's about the way I am. It hurts too much sometimes, but—"

"One thing's for sure. You're *going* to grow up, and Jeff's going to see one day what a fine-looking young lady you are. You already are, as far as I'm concerned."

"I'll never be as pretty as Sarah."

Tom looked at her quickly. His mouth tightened into a straight line, and he said no more.

Leah knew that she had said too much, for Tom was sensitive about speaking of Sarah. "Look," she said, "there's the church tower right over there! See it?"

"Yep, we'll be at the station in five minutes."

His prediction was accurate. The train huffed and chuffed as it slowed down. When they pulled into the station, it expelled a great gust of steam.

"Guess we better get our stuff together," Tom said. He stood up, balancing for a moment.

Leah saw that it pained him to stand. But she said nothing, for she knew he was sensitive about the leg too. As the train came to a clanking stop, she picked up Esther. "If you'll get the suitcases, I can handle her."

"All right."

They stepped off the train, and at once Tom was gripped by his father, who suddenly appeared right beside him.

"Tom!" he said. "By Harry, it's good to see you again! You're looking fine!"

Tom swallowed hard and hugged his father, then stepped back. His father was in military dress, and Tom was wearing the uniform he had worn at Gettysburg—which had been patched together by Sarah. "I guess it must look funny—a colonel hugging a sergeant!"

"Who cares!" his father said. "Now, let me look at this girl of mine." He took the child from Leah and held her carefully in his arms. "Hello, Esther," he said quietly, his eyes going over her face. "Aren't you the pretty one?"

Leah watched, afraid that Esther would cry. She was not used to strangers and was somewhat shy. However, something in her father's voice must have calmed her, for she suddenly smiled and reached out to touch his mustache.

"She looks just like your mother, Tom," Colonel Majors said, stroking the golden hair with his free hand. "She's going to be as pretty as she was."

Leah felt like crying over the sadness of the situation, but she knew that would not do. She stood quietly until the colonel said, "Well, suppose we get you three settled. You're going out to Silas's place. You'll have it all to yourself. He's gone to visit a friend of his."

"He must be doing better then," Leah said with some surprise. Uncle Silas had not been in good health when she had left Richmond, and she had worried about him.

"He seems to get stronger all the time. I'm real proud of him," Nelson Majors said. "Come on. I've commandeered an army ambulance. What's the use of being a colonel if you can't break the rules once in a while?"

They got in, and he said, "I've got to go by the camp before we leave. There's something I have to take care of. Besides, I want to show off my daughter to the general."

Leah and Tom sat quietly in the back of the ambulance as a corporal drove them to the army camp. On the way, Tom's eyes ran over the rows of men drilling in an open field. If he thought about never being able to march again, if he felt useless and helpless, he said nothing.

At headquarters they were greeted by Gen. A. P. Hill himself. The general was delighted with Esther. "She's the finest young'un I've ever seen, Colonel!" he said when Esther allowed him to pick her up.

"Thank you, General," Colonel Majors said. "I believe you know my son, Tom."

"Why, indeed I do. You've spoken enough of him," Hill said. He took Tom's salute, then stuck his hand out. "Glad you're back, Sergeant. Will you be coming back on active duty?"

"No, sir, unless you can find a place for a one-legged man."

"Why, I expect we can do that! General Hood lost an arm *and* a leg, and he's still commanding like he always was." He nodded at Tom's father. "See if you can't find a place for him. I know you'd like that, Colonel."

After the general left, Tom said, "Where's Jeff, Pa—I mean, Colonel?"

"He would have been here himself, but we didn't know exactly when you were getting in," his father said. "There's some kind of a traveling show in town." He grinned. "Jeff thought he had to see it."

"What kind of a show?"

"I don't know! Some sort of minstrel show, I suppose. He pestered me until I let him go." He glanced at Leah, and a thought seemed to come to him. "Why don't you go down and find him, Leah? Then he can bring you out to Silas's place. I'll see that he gets a wagon from the quartermaster."

"Oh, that would be nice!"

"We'll drop you off downtown, then. Come along!"

Leah climbed back into the wagon, and soon they were making their way through the streets of Richmond. She noticed that the city had become shabby and dilapidated. With no new supplies coming in for repairs, and no time or effort available for paint or cleanup, the city looked stark and ragged, like an old beggar who had no one to care for him.

"Place looks pretty run-down, sir," Tom said as they rumbled along.

"I guess it does, but it's still here. The Union's done everything they could to take it."

Tom smiled at this. "I heard another story about Lincoln. Somebody came in and wanted a pass for Richmond, and he said, 'Well, I gave passes to Richmond to General McClellan, and he hasn't been able to get there with a hundred thousand men, but maybe you can do it by yourself.'"

Colonel Majors laughed. "I wish our president had a sense of humor like Lincoln's." He pointed. "There's the theater, Leah, and the show's probably already started. Maybe you just want to wait until it lets out, and then you can see Jeff."

"I think I'll do that." Leah got to the ground and waved good-bye, then took up a waiting place beside the theater. She asked once how long the show would be, and the ticket taker said, "Won't be more than ten minutes more. Another show will be starting right away."

"Thank you."

Soon people began coming out. Anxiously she searched the crowd, for it occurred to her that if she missed Jeff she would be stranded alone in Richmond with no way to get to Uncle Silas's but by walking.

And then she spotted his black hair above the gray uniform as he emerged. He seemed to have grown since she had seen him last! She started forward and opened her lips to cry, "Jeff, here I am!" But then she stopped.

By Jeff's side was Lucy Driscoll, dressed in a peach-colored gown and her hair done up in the latest style. She looked as pretty as any girl Leah had ever seen, and she was hanging onto Jeff's arm. Lucy was small, as Leah had always wanted to be. Now, as she looked up and laughed into Jeff's eyes, there was a flirtatious manner about her that Leah knew she herself could never achieve.

The pair drew closer, and once again Leah started to speak. But before she could, Lucy reached up, pulled Jeff's head down, and gave him a kiss on the cheek.

Jeff flushed but seemed pleased by it all, and at that moment he saw Leah. He swallowed hard and stopped abruptly. "Why, look, Lucy. There's Leah!" He came up to her at once but looked somewhat discomfited. "I didn't expect you *today!*" he said awkwardly. Lucy was still hanging onto his right arm, so he disengaged it and held out his hand. "Good to see you, Leah."

Leah took his hand but shook it only briefly. "I didn't mean to interrupt," she said rather coldly.

"Your father has taken Esther and Tom out to Uncle Silas's."

"Why didn't you go along with them?" Lucy said. "I'd think you'd want to."

Leah wanted to say, "I wanted to be with Jeff," but she did not want to admit that.

"Well, I'll take you out there, Leah. Lucy and I will, won't we?"

"Of course, we'll be glad to. My father will have a carriage take us."

"Your father said for you to come in one of the army wagons, Jeff," Leah said. She looked at Lucy. "But he doesn't have to go if he doesn't want to."

Jeff said quickly, "Well, of course I want to!" He turned back to Lucy. "Look, there's Samson over there. You don't mind if he takes you home, do you, Lucy?"

As a matter of fact, Lucy probably did mind. But it was obvious she saw there was no other way out. "Of course not, and, Leah, you must come over to see us. Jeff comes to our house quite often, don't you, Jeff?"

Jeff looked rather foolish and said, "Why, I guess I do."

"Thank you." Leah waited until the two had said their good-byes.

Jeff turned to her then, saying, "I guess we'll have to walk out to the camp and pick up a wagon."

"I guess so."

On the walk to the army camp, Jeff asked about Esther, then about all of Leah's people back in Kentucky. He noticed quickly that she was unusually silent, and he asked, "Is something wrong? Did you get sick on the train?"

"No, not at all!"

"Well, you just look sort of pale." Then he added, "But you look good. You've grown up even in the little time you've been gone." He almost said, "I'm glad you're back," but Leah was acting so strangely that he could not think of a way to put it.

At last, when they had obtained the wagon and were on their way out of town toward Uncle Silas's farm, he said, "You're not upset with me because I went to the play with Lucy, are you?"

"You can go to a play with anybody you want to," she said. "I'm not your keeper!"

Instantly Jeff knew she was upset, but there was nothing he could do about it now. He spoke to the horses and drove off at a fast clip. He was thinking, *Girls sure are funny. I wish they'd be nice and steady like boys.*

4
Lady with a Temper

I don't see why she has to get so mad! After all, it was only an old show!"

Tom Majors looked across the field desk at Jeff. Tom had become an aide to his father, had procured a new uniform, and looked very handsome. A week had passed since he'd arrived in Richmond with Leah and Esther, and during that time he had noticed that Jeff was getting grumpier and grumpier.

Putting his turkey-quill pen down, Tom leaned back in his chair and studied his younger brother. "You'll have to remember that girls have sensitive feelings," he remarked.

Jeff lifted his heavy eyebrows in a gesture of surprise. "Well, what about me? Don't you think I've got any feelings?"

Tom grinned abruptly. "No, I don't think boys are supposed to have feelings. They're like pigs and dogs. They don't really get angry or upset or get their feelings hurt."

"What are you talking about? Even dogs get their feelings hurt. I remember the time you fussed at Old Blue for not treeing any squirrels, and he went around for a week with his tail between his legs."

"Yes, but Blue was an unusual dog. He was far more sensitive than you are, Jeff. You're supposed to be a tough Confederate soldier, and here you are worried about little things like your girl being mad at you."

"She's not my girl!" Jeff said and clenched his teeth. "We're just good friends, so I don't see why she has to get mad at me just because I took Lucy Driscoll to an old minstrel show!"

Tom picked up the turkey quill and dipped it into the ink. He stared at the pen and said, "Did you know that right-handed people have to have quills from the right wing of the turkey in order to make the ink flow right?"

Jeff stared at his brother as if he had lost his mind. "Tom, here I am having a crisis, and you're giving me a lecture on which side of a turkey wing a quill comes out of! Who cares? What I want to know is, how am I gonna talk sense into Leah!"

"Why don't you give her a present? Some candy or some perfume or something like that would be good."

Jeff paused and thought about it. "Nah, that wouldn't work."

"How do you know?"

"Because I already tried it."

Jeff stood up and stomped out of the tent, leaving Tom half amused and half troubled over his younger brother's problems. He wrote steadily for some time, and then his father came in. Tom stood to his feet, saluting him sharply. "Good morning, Colonel Majors!"

"Good morning, Sergeant!" The colonel looked approvingly at his son's natty new uniform. "That's probably one of the last new uniforms in the whole Confederacy. It looks a whole lot better than mine."

Tom looked down self-consciously. "I feel like a

fake, really. Wearing a uniform when I know I'm not going to be doing any fighting."

Nelson Majors sat on a camp chair and looked over the work that Tom was doing. "It takes more than people shooting guns to win a war. You know that, Tom. Somebody's got to make the guns and the bullets—and get them to the front. You've been a great help to me since you've come back. It's going to be a real job to get this army ready to face Grant." Leaning back in his chair, he brushed a hand over his coal-black hair. "People never think about how hard it is to move ten thousand men from point A to point B."

"Especially when most of the railroads aren't working, and we don't have any horses."

"Right! Now, Stonewall Jackson, he was a genius at that sort of thing."

Tom grinned ruefully. "Yep, if he didn't kill us first, he'd get us to where he wanted us, all right. That man sure didn't have any patience with anybody who dropped by the way."

"No, he didn't. He was tough—but the best general that I ever saw."

"Better than General Lee?"

"He was General Lee's right arm. But he couldn't do what Lee's doing, like making things smooth with President Jeff Davis. Talk about somebody having sensitive feelings! Our president's as sensitive as a man without a skin."

Tom blinked. "Oh, that reminds me. Jeff and Leah are still carrying on with that feud of theirs."

"They'll get over it."

"Sure, I know that, and you know that, but Jeff doesn't know that. He thinks it's going on forever. Growing up is pretty hard, Colonel."

Nelson Majors looked over at his tall son and smiled briefly. "I don't know if I'll ever get either of you raised." He hesitated, then added, "You haven't said anything about Sarah since you've been back."

"Yes, I have. I told you she was doing well."

"That's not telling me about her."

Tom knew exactly what his father wanted to know, but he did not choose to talk about it. He also knew he would have to sooner or later, but now he just said shortly, "We're not engaged, Pa."

"I thought you wanted to marry her."

"I don't want her to marry a man with only one leg. She deserves better than that."

"That's her decision, Tom, not yours."

Tom looked at his father with surprise. He respected his father's opinion greatly. "Well, Pa," he said lamely, "I just don't want to handicap her."

"Suppose *she'd* lost a leg. Would you still want her?"

"Why, of course I would, but that's different."

"It's not a bit different!" Nelson Majors argued. "Love is more than an arm or a leg. It's for better or for worse."

"Well, if an accident comes *after* marriage, that's true. But there are lots of men that would like to marry Sarah, and she deserves the best."

"I think *you* are the best, Tom, and you ought to give this matter serious thought."

"Well, I don't—"

"I'm looking for Colonel Nelson Majors!"

Both men looked up as a woman appeared almost magically at the opening of the tent. She was not a large woman, and she was not more than twenty-seven or twenty-eight, Tom estimated. And she was very pretty. She had bright red hair and

43

eyes a strange shade of blue-green. Her face was oval, and she had a dimple in her right cheek even when she wasn't smiling—and she wasn't smiling now. There was an angry look on her face.

The colonel said, "I'm Colonel Majors. May I help you?"

"I want to speak to you—alone!"

"Sergeant, would you leave us alone?"

"Yes, sir!"

As soon as Tom was out of the room, Nelson Majors said, "Will you have a seat, Miss . . ."

"It's *Mrs.* Mrs. Eileen Fremont, and I don't need a seat to tell you what's on my mind!"

Nelson had been admiring the beauty of the woman, for she was indeed very attractive. However, he felt uncomfortable with the anger he saw in her eyes. "What's troubling you, Mrs. Fremont?"

"I've come to complain about the way my brother-in-law is being treated."

"Brother-in-law?"

"Yes, he's in Libby Prison here in Richmond. I've come all the way from Louisiana to see him."

"Your brother-in-law was in the *Federal* Army?"

"Yes, he was!" Eileen Fremont's chin rose in determination. "There are quite a few of us from the South who have relatives in the Yankee army."

"I understand, Mrs. Fremont. I come from Kentucky myself, and many of my friends and some of my family decided to stay in the Union."

"Have you been to Libby Prison, Colonel?"

"No, ma'am."

"It's a disgrace! They treat the men there worse than we treat pigs back in Louisiana! Men are sleeping on the ground without a single blanket! The

44

place is filled with lice, and the food isn't fit to feed a hog!"

Nelson Majors felt definitely ill at ease. "Well, I'm sorry to hear that, Mrs. Fremont. But actually that's out of my department. You will have to see the head of the prison—"

"I've tried to see him, but he won't let me in!"

"I expect he's very busy."

Mrs. Fremont's eyes glinted. "I saw him at a restaurant. He was eating himself into the grave. He's fat as a pig, and he looks, more or less, like one!"

"Did you speak to him, Mrs. Fremont?"

"I walked right up to him and told him what I thought, with everybody in the restaurant listening." A smile touched her lips briefly. "He wouldn't see me in his office, so I had to see him wherever I could."

Nelson found the scene amusing but did not allow that to show on his face. "What did he say?"

"He told me to get out of the restaurant. That I was nothing but a Yankee sympathizer. When I refused to go, he asked the manager to take me out. Which he did."

Nelson hesitated. This was far outside his sphere, and he was burdened with the responsibility of getting men ready to fight. He knew from rumor that the prisons in the South *were* bad, and he was aware that those in the North were equally bad. He tried to explain this to the woman, but she stood, feet planted, eyes glinting, simply waiting for him to finish.

Finally he said, "So you see, Mrs. Fremont, there's nothing much I can do to help you. Perhaps

I could give you a note to give to the commander of the prisons—"

"And what good would that do?"

In all fairness, he knew that it would do no good at all. "The problem," he said, "is that we're having trouble feeding ourselves, Mrs. Fremont. So, of course, we have little food to spare—or blankets either, for that matter. Perhaps I could help your brother-in-law a little. I believe I could scare up a blanket or two."

His offer seemed to ease some of the fury in her eyes. Still, her lips were tightly pressed together. She said, "It's going to take more than a blanket. He's very sick, and he's going to die if he doesn't get help. He needs to be in a hospital."

"I'm sure that's been considered—"

"*Considered?* A man's dying, and you're *considering* whether to put him in the hospital?" Eileen Fremont's eyes lit up again, and for the next five minutes she told Colonel Majors exactly what she thought of him, of the whole Confederate prison system, of Jefferson Davis, and of everyone else. Finally she said, "I'm sure nothing will come of this, so no thanks to you, Colonel!" She turned and stalked out of the tent.

As soon as she disappeared, Tom came back in, his eyes wide with astonishment. "That lady sure knows how to say what she means, doesn't she?"

At that instant Lieutenant Logan stepped inside, a grin on his face. "I caught the last of that one, Colonel. I think I'd rather face Yankee cannons than a lady like that!"

"The woman's unreasonable!" Colonel Majors said. His feelings had been scraped raw by her

46

accusations. "What does she expect me to do? I expect she's just a Yankee sympathizer."

"No, I know a little bit about her," the lieutenant said. "She's been waiting around the prison. I was there the other day talking to one of the guards. He told me about her."

"What did he say?"

"Actually, it's pretty sad. Her husband joined up at Bull Run, and he got killed at Shiloh, so she's a widow. I guess she and her brother-in-law were pretty close. She's for the South all right, but she's one pretty tough lady."

"I never could stand a woman with a temper," Colonel Majors said.

"Well, sir, you'd better get used to this one because she'll probably be back."

"I hope not! If she does, just tell her that I'm kept pretty busy, will you, Sergeant?"

"I'll tell her, Colonel," Tom said. "But she doesn't seem to me like the kind of woman that would listen to a lowly sergeant."

Nelson Majors looked at his son quickly to see if he was being ridiculed, but he could see nothing on Tom's smooth face. "Well, I'm sorry for her, but there's nothing I can do. If she comes back, try to shift her off to somebody else, all right?"

"Yes, sir, I'll do all I can."

Later, when he was explaining all this to Jeff, Tom said, "I never saw Pa so shook up. He can face a charge with bare bayonets, but that little red-haired lady sure did shake him up."

"I'd like to have seen that." Jeff grinned. "Maybe he'd understand my problems with Leah a little better."

"I don't think Leah ever loses her temper like this woman did. I'll tell you what—she came in there looking like a bear. A pretty bear, I must admit, but all the same I hope she doesn't show up again."

5

Wanted: One Mother

Colonel Majors was busy from morning till late at night attending to the thousand details necessary to put an army in the field. Word had come from General Lee to bring up at once whatever forces were available. The city of Richmond was scoured for ammunition, uniforms, horses. The countryside gave up whatever food was available, and slowly the army began to take shape.

Nelson Majors, for all his activity, never completely forgot his daughter. Constantly he was wondering what would happen to Esther if he lost his life on the field of battle. He said nothing to his sons about this but spent as much time as possible trying to plan some way to protect the child in case something happened to him.

One Tuesday morning, when he had time to breathe from his duties, he went for a walk. Out by the edge of the camp there was a small creek that he liked to sit beside and listen to the water gurgle over the stones. It was very quiet as he walked along, watching the schools of minnows flash like silver in the shallow stream. From time to time a frog would cry out and splash into the water. Overhead the trees were green, and it was cool under their shade, even though the temperature in the sun was almost one hundred.

He sat on a large rock, where he prayed and thought and pondered over what could be done. As he did so, an idea that he'd had almost from the day Esther arrived began to take form in his mind. It seemed difficult to put into operation, but now, taking a deep breath, he stood up and said, "But I've got to do *something!*" He walked quickly back to camp.

As soon as the colonel entered his tent, Tom stood to his feet. He must have seen something in his father's face, for he asked, "What is it, Pa?"

"I've been thinking about Esther. We'll be leaving here, Tom—very soon. You'll go with me and so will Jeff. I just can't leave Esther alone with Leah out there."

"She hasn't said anything about going home yet."

"I know, but she's too young to have such responsibility."

"I guess she is, although she's very grown up in many ways." Tom studied his father, then said, "You're not going to send them back to Kentucky, are you?"

"No, I don't want to do that, but I do have another idea. It may be difficult though."

"What is it, Pa?" Tom simply could not call his father "Colonel" every time he addressed him. "Pa" just seemed to slip out from time to time. "I mean Colonel," he said.

Nelson grinned at his son. "Hard to get used to, isn't it? Well, Sergeant, here's my idea. I think we're going to have to hire someone as a sort of a mother for Esther."

"A mother? How could that be?"

"Well, maybe not a mother. Let's say a housekeeper. Esther needs a grown woman around, and

Leah can't be tied to her all the time. She's got to have some relief."

"I think that's right. That's a good idea, Pa!"

"It's the best I could come up with. Do you know anybody around here that might do that sort of thing?"

"Well, no, but then, I just got back from Kentucky. Maybe one of the officers has an older daughter . . ."

"Not that I know of." Colonel Majors sat down and thought hard. He said, "I thought we might advertise."

"You mean put it in the paper?"

"Well, the paper doesn't come out too regularly now. What I thought is, we'd make a notice and put it up in several places around town—at the post office and the general store—places like that."

"That's a good idea, sir. Why don't you write it, and I'll carry them around?"

"Let's both write. I'll make the first draft, and you can make copies. We ought to have at least ten."

"You make the first one, and I'll copy the rest," Tom said, glad to have something to do. He, too, had been worried about leaving Esther and Leah alone, and he began speaking optimistically as his father wrote the notice. "Why, it won't be hard. There are lots of women in Richmond. Lots of widows, I'm sorry to say. How much would we pay?"

"As much as we have to," his father said. He finished the notice and held it out. "Do you think that will do?"

Tom read it aloud: "Wanted: One mature lady to keep three-year-old child for officer who will be leaving Richmond temporarily. Apply to Colonel Nelson Majors."

"That ought to do it!" Tom said eagerly. "Let me copy these, and I'll post them all over town."

Colonel Majors rose and looked out the tent flap at the activity outside. "This better work, Tom. We're not going to be here long."

Tom pressured Jeff into helping him, and together the two of them made thirty copies of the notice. Dividing them with Jeff, he said, "You take the north part of town, and I'll take the south part. Be sure you put them up where they'll be seen."

"Sure, Tom, I'll take care of it."

Jeff grabbed the announcements and made off for town. He made sure to get permission from the storekeepers at the busiest stores, and he found they were all willing. Some said they would even urge people to look into the ad. One of them, a clothing store owner, said, "Bound to be plenty of ladies who'll take care of a girl for an officer in our glorious army."

"Well, just send them on to my pa, Colonel Majors," Jeff said.

Afterward, he wandered around town, having a little free time, As he turned the corner to go down Elm Street, he came face to face with Leah. "Why— hello, Leah," he said. "I didn't expect to see you here."

"I drove the wagon in to see if we could find some supplies." Her voice was chilly.

"Be better off to go around to farmhouses," Jeff said. "The stores here sell out as quick as they get anything."

"Oh, I didn't think about that!"

"Let me go with you. I'll drive the wagon, and I bet we can find all that you need."

"You don't have to do that."

"I'd like to do it. Come on. Where's the wagon?"

All afternoon the two drove down country lanes, stopping at farmhouses, and as Jeff had said, food was easier to buy from farmers than from stores.

It was toward the end of the afternoon when Jeff put into the wagon the last of the fresh corn Leah had managed to buy. He said, "Well, it's getting late. And I guess I better get back to camp."

Leah had softened somewhat during the afternoon, and some hint of the old relationship she had with Jeff seemed to be coming back. "I guess I'd better be getting home too."

"I wish I could go with you, but they might post me as a deserter."

"Oh, they wouldn't do that. Not with you being the colonel's son."

"I guess not." Jeff grinned. "Here, let me help you into the wagon."

Leah seemed surprised. She took his hand, however, and as she climbed in, he squeezed it.

Then he walked around and clambered up to sit beside her. Taking up the lines, he said, "Get up, boys!" He turned to Leah and asked, "So my baby sister's doing all right?"

"She's fine, Jeff. She's the best little girl that there ever was. I know Ma and Sarah and Morena are missing her like everything. And Pa too. He really dotes on her."

The horses' hooves made a plodding sound and raised the dust as they went along the road toward camp. Far overhead, a flock of red-winged blackbirds made their noisy way to alight in a cornfield. Watching them, Jeff said, "You remember the time we shot a bunch of red-winged blackbirds, and you cooked 'em up, and we ate 'em?"

Leah smiled. "I remember. It was out at the foot of Little Mountain. Also we stayed out too long, and your pa sent Tom to get us. I think that was one of the few times my pa ever paddled me."

"You shoulda got what I got." Jeff winced. "Pa didn't look kindly on that."

They rode along slowly as the sun sank. A cool breeze sprang up, and Jeff took off his hat and put it on the seat between them. "I wish we were back in Kentucky, and this whole war had never come along."

"So do I. But I guess people everywhere in this country are wishing that."

"Well, maybe after this next battle it'll all be over."

"I hope so," Leah said.

When they reached camp, Jeff got out of Leah's wagon and handed the lines to her. "You may have some company pretty soon, Leah. I forgot to tell you. Pa's trying to hire a lady to come out and help you take care of Esther."

"Why, I don't need any help!"

"I know you can take care of her good, but two of you would be better. If one of you had to go to town, don't you see? It would be easier than trying to find a neighbor to help out—like today."

"I suppose that's true."

Jeff hesitated. "Were you thinkin' of going back to Kentucky?"

Leah glanced quickly at him. "I'm not going until I'm sure Esther has good care."

Jeff grinned suddenly. "That's good." He stood by the wagon for a few more moments. "I'd hate to see you go back," he said awkwardly. "I missed you."

"You didn't miss me very much, Jeff! You had Lucy to keep you company!"

Jeff's face clouded. The specter of Lucy Driscoll again. "For crying out loud, Leah! Are you never going to forget about that? I just took her to an old minstrel show!"

"That wasn't the only time you took her somewhere, was it?" she said sharply.

Jeff kicked at a clod of dirt and kept his head down. "Well, a fella's got to do something."

"Well, you just go ahead, Jeff, and do something! See if I care!"

He turned away abruptly, and Leah spoke to the horses, who lunged against their collars. The two parted, Jeff feeling about as bad as he could. He wondered, *Why did she have to act like that?*

Nelson Majors looked up. The corporal on guard duty was standing just inside the tent door.

"There's a lady here to see you, sir."

"Well, show her in, Corporal."

"Yes, sir."

The colonel put down the book he had been reading. He rose out of his chair and said as a woman entered, "Well, good afternoon—" But then the woman lifted her head, and he ended lamely, "Oh, it's you, Mrs. Fremont!" He braced himself for what he expected was coming. "I trust your brother-in-law is better?"

"He's dead, Colonel."

Eileen Fremont's voice was so calm that at first Nelson Majors could not believe he had heard correctly, but then, seeing the pain in the woman's eyes, he knew that he had. "I'm very sorry to hear that, Mrs. Fremont."

"He developed blood poisoning, and there was nothing they could do for him."

Again the colonel could only say, "I offer you my sincerest sympathy."

Mrs. Fremont was silent for several seconds. Then, looking up at the tall officer, she said, "They told me that you visited him in the hospital, and that you spoke to the doctors to get him better care."

"Well, yes, ma'am, I did do that."

"It was kind of you."

"I wish I could've done more." The colonel shifted on his feet, not knowing what else to say. "Will you be going back to Louisiana, Mrs. Fremont, after your brother-in-law's funeral?"

"The funeral was this morning. I've come about another matter, sir."

"Another matter? What could that be?"

"About this notice." Mrs. Fremont pulled a paper out of her reticule, the small purse carried by most ladies in the South, and held it up. "I've come to tell you that I'm taking the position."

Nelson Majors had turned down three applicants already—they had been hard-looking women, he thought—and now he was quite prepared to turn down another one. He had seen Eileen Fremont's temper and was not at all certain that she would be the suitable woman to care for Esther.

"Well, sit down, Mrs. Fremont, and we can talk about it."

The woman took her seat, folded her hands in her lap, and said calmly, "How old is your daughter, Colonel?"

"Three years old. Her mother died when she was born."

"I'm very sorry, Colonel."

Almost desperately the colonel searched his mind, trying to figure out some way to put this woman out of his office. Finally he had what he thought was a fine idea. "I would expect that the woman who takes care of my daughter knows something about children—I mean, she should have had some experience."

"I had a daughter, Colonel," Mrs. Fremont said quietly. When the colonel simply looked questioningly at her, she said, "She died when she was just about the age of your daughter. She was two and a half. She died right after my husband fell at Shiloh."

"Oh, I see." It sounded trite to say, "I'm sorry," over and over again, but Nelson Majors was conscious of a swift streak of pity for this woman. To have lost her husband and her only child so close together was a tragedy indeed. "That was very hard," he said gently. "But won't your family be looking for you back in Louisiana?"

"I have very little family, Colonel. I will be all right here. As a matter of fact, I prefer not to go back."

"This isn't exactly a health resort. Richmond is the target of all the Union armies. It may be invaded."

"Well do I know that, Colonel!" Eileen Fremont did not seem troubled. She sat watching him, studying him. "Is there something about me that you dislike, Colonel? Is there some reason why you would not want me to be around your daughter?"

"Why, no, of course not . . . that is . . ." Nelson

stumbled painfully, then he said with a shrug, "Well, you do have a temper."

"Yes, I do, and from what I hear from your men, you do too!"

Taken aback, he could only laugh. "You're right there. I do have a temper, and you were perfectly right to be angry about the way your brother-in-law was being treated."

"What exactly would you want from the woman you hire?"

"I'll be leaving soon with the regiment. I don't know when I'll be back. I have two sons, Tom and Jeff, both in the army in my command. We'll all be gone, but we don't know for how long. My daughter's being kept at a small house outside of town by a young woman—very young. Her name's Leah Carter. Her family's kept my daughter until now. We were good neighbors back in Kentucky." He went on to explain that he had felt it was wrong for his daughter not to know her father or her brothers. He ended by saying sadly, "We may have done the wrong thing in sending for her, for here I have to go off to battle right away."

Eileen Fremont said softly, "I think it was a noble gesture, Colonel. A man wants to see his children. If you would like for me to go with you and let your daughter see if she would like me, I would be glad to."

"That's a good idea." Nelson Majors got up at once and grabbed his hat. "Come along. I'll take you to her."

He commandeered a wagon from the quartermaster, helped Mrs. Fremont in, and then climbed up beside her. "I'll be gone for an hour or perhaps more, Private," he said. "Would you pass that word along to my officers?"

He then spoke to the horses, who stepped out with a sprightly gait. A cloud of dust began to gather behind them.

"It's a rough ride, Mrs. Fremont."

"I don't mind."

The colonel glanced at the woman beside him. He had already noted that she was very attractive. She wore a light gray silk dress that fitted her well and on her head a white, woven hat tied by a ribbon under her chin. He wondered about her age, and finally he thought it would not be wrong to ask. "What is your age, Mrs. Fremont?"

"I'm twenty-eight."

She said no more until they were halfway to the house. Then she turned to him. "I very much appreciate what you did for my brother-in-law. You have a kind heart, Colonel Majors."

Her words lifted the colonel's spirits. "I wish I could have done more," he said again.

They talked more easily after that, and Nelson Majors found himself thinking, *I believe this one will do. If Esther likes her, she's the closest thing I can find to giving her a mother—at least for a while.*

6
Boys Are Pretty Silly

Esther whirled across the floor, holding her arms out to keep her balance. Her chubby arms and legs were dimpled, and her blonde hair fell around her face in ringlets. She tripped suddenly and fell on her face.

Leah dropped her sewing and crossed the room to pick up the little girl, saying, "Be careful! You'll hurt yourself."

Esther said, "No, not hurt!" and grinned happily, showing bright new teeth. "Outside!" she said, pulling vigorously at Leah's dress.

"No, we can't go outside now. I've got to start fixing supper." She gave Esther a squeeze. "You always want to go outside. Maybe after supper I'll take you out for a walk. Maybe we'll see a bird."

"See bird!" Esther echoed. She had taken to repeating everything she heard and was rapidly learning to put sentences together. "Esther go see bird!"

"That's right, but after supper."

The child seemed satisfied, and she toddled into the kitchen after Leah, generally making a pest out of herself as Leah began to pull the materials together for the evening meal. Then she said, "Horses!" and ran out of the room.

Startled, Leah put down the sifter on the table and went into the hallway. She saw Esther push against the screen door and was glad it was locked. "Wait a minute, Esther!" she cried.

When she reached the door, Leah saw that it was Jeff, riding a horse with a Confederate cavalry saddle. Unlocking the screen, she grabbed Esther and stepped outside. "Jeff!" she cried. "What are you doing here?"

Jeff slipped off the horse expertly and tied the animal to the hitching post. "I came to see my baby sister. How are you, Esther?"

"Jeff! Jeff!" Esther ran across the porch and would have fallen down the steps if he had not leaped forward and caught her.

"Hold on there, sister!" he said. "You're gonna skin your nose."

He spun her around, and the child laughed with delight. She pulled at his hair, demanding that he play horsey with her as he always did.

"Can you stay for supper, Jeff?"

Jeff held Esther in his arms and looked over at Leah as though he never knew how to take her. "I guess so, if it won't be any trouble. I'll go down and fish in the pond while you're cooking."

"Take Esther with you, but be sure she doesn't fall in."

"Why, I wouldn't allow a thing like that!" Jeff threw Esther up in the air, and she squealed.

"Again! Again, Jeff!" she said.

"If I finish, I'll come down and watch you," Leah said.

"Sure. I'll take your pole too, in case you have time to fish a little."

Jeff went by the barn, leading Esther by the hand. She would have stumbled, but he kept pulling

61

her up and laughing at her. "Come on now—you can walk better than that!"

Ten minutes later they were at the small pond behind the house. It was no more than thirty feet across, but it was filled with plump, small panfish. Jeff put Esther down and said, "Now, don't you fall in the water."

"Fall in the water!" Esther said happily. She sat down at once and began digging in the dirt.

Jeff watched her, grinned, then said, "Go on, get dirty. See if I care!" He baited a hook, swung the line up, and watched the cork float on the smooth surface. He watched Esther too, but she made no move to go toward the water. He got a bite, pulled a fish in, and showed it to the child. "Look, that's a punkinseed perch," he said. "We'll have him for supper tonight, maybe."

Esther reached out to touch the fish. Just as she did, it flopped out of Jeff's hand, and her eyes went big with astonishment. Her lips trembled, and she began to cry.

"That's just an old fish, Esther. Look!" He picked it up and put her tiny, fat forefinger on it. "See—it won't hurt you."

"Hurt Esther."

"No, it can't hurt you. Look, we'll put this one on a stringer, and we'll catch another one."

For an hour, Jeff played with Esther and caught a few sun perch. Then he looked up to see Leah coming down the path toward the pond. "I got enough for supper," he said when she stopped. "Do you want to fish awhile?"

"No, I'll just watch."

He fixed his eyes on the cork. It had always been easy to talk to Leah, but that was not true any longer. Desperately he wondered what to say to her. Finally he asked, "Have you seen Cecil Taylor?"

"Just once. He came by the other day. He was with Lucy."

"Oh!" Jeff had not wanted to bring up Lucy since she had been the cause of all the difficulty with Leah. Immediately he changed the subject. "Esther looks pretty! Is that a new dress she's got?"

"Yes, I made it myself."

"You did?" Jeff looked at it closely. "Well, isn't that fine? I knew you could sew, but not this well."

"It's not hard to make a dress for a little one."

Somehow their argument had frozen her up, or so it seemed. She sat looking across the pond. A snake swam from one spot to another, making a V-shaped ripple. It was headed away from them, but she warned Jeff anyway. "Look, there's a snake! I wouldn't want one to get to Esther."

Jeff lifted his head. "Just a water snake," he said calmly. "He wouldn't hurt anybody."

"All snakes are alike to me. I'm afraid of all of them."

Jeff began to talk about snakes. He cast his eyes secretly upon Leah, who sat facing the water. He admired the smooth turn of her cheek and noticed that her eyelashes seemed thicker than ever. *She sure is getting pretty,* he thought. *But I wouldn't dare tell her so. She'd bite my head off.*

This was not the first argument he had had with Leah. Their disagreements were usually over little things, but they had never stayed angry this long before. At least *she* was angry.

Then Jeff talked about how it had been back in Kentucky. He did this often, for that had been the most pleasant time of his life. "You remember Ol' Napoleon?"

"I certainly do!"

Napoleon was the huge bass that lived in a stream not far from Jeff's old home place. He and Leah had spent a lot of time trying to catch that fish, but he was a wily breed.

Thinking of Napoleon, Leah seemed to relax slightly. "You remember we did catch him once? Then you let him go. I never did know why you did that, Jeff."

"Oh, I don't know." He picked up a stone, looked at it, skimmed it across the water. It hopped four times, then sank quietly. Turning to look at her, he said, "I guess I just wanted to keep something the same. Everything else has changed, it seems like, and I wanted Ol' Napoleon to be there when the war's over."

"I hope he *is* still there. I went down there just before I came back to Richmond, but I didn't see him."

"Sure hope somebody hasn't caught him. I'm the one who wants to do that!"

"We will! As soon as the war's over and you come back."

Jeff glanced at her. She seemed somehow not quite so upset today. Feeling better, he said, "What would you do with him, Leah, if we caught him?"

That thought apparently had never occurred to her. "Why, I don't know."

Jeff teased her. "Would you eat him?"

"Eat Napoleon? Why, that would be like being a cannibal!"

"Well, we could have him stuffed. Then every time we'd look up on the wall, we'd see Ol' Napoleon and think about when we were kids fishing for him together."

Leah laughed. It was the first time Jeff had heard her laugh since she had come back from Kentucky.

"I don't think I could stand to see Ol' Napoleon all stuffed," she said.

"Well, then, we could get a big barrel and keep him in it. But it wouldn't be right to keep a fish in a barrel either. They need to be free. I guess we'll just go down to the creek and visit him."

"Jeff . . ." Leah began uncertainly.

Was she was going to say, "I've been so foolish, and I'm sorry"? If so, she did not have the chance.

"Leah," a voice called. "Come back to the house —and bring Esther."

Jeff looked up. "Why, that's Pa, and he's got somebody with him. We better get back there."

He stood and grabbed the string of fish and the poles as Leah picked up Esther. "I bet I know who that is," he said as they started for the house.

"The woman? Who is she?"

"I better let Pa tell you."

When they reached the house, Leah looked at the stranger and then at Colonel Majors. "Hello, Colonel!" she said.

"Hello, Leah. I brought somebody I'd like you to meet." Turning, he said, "This is Eileen Fremont." He looked back to Leah. "This is Leah Carter. She's been the next thing to a mother for Esther ever since she was born. Leah, Mrs. Fremont's going to help you take care of Esther."

Leah lowered Esther to the floor, Colonel Majors reached down, and the child flew to him. "Papa! Papa!" She patted him on the cheek.

65

Leah had no time to say anything,

"Esther, this is Mrs. Fremont."

Esther looked up at the woman but held tightly to her father. Her eyes grew big, and she said, "Hello."

Eileen Fremont smiled at her. "You're a pretty baby, Esther. Would you let me hold you?"

"No, Papa hold!"

Eileen Fremont laughed at that. "Well, I can see she's attached to her father. Give me a day or two, and I think she'll come to me."

"I brought Mrs. Fremont to meet Esther to see if they could get along," the colonel explained to Leah. "Jeff, Tom, and I will be leaving pretty soon, and we thought you could use some company in the house and some help with Esther."

"That'll be fine, Colonel."

"You won't mind having me on your hands, will you, Leah?" Mrs. Fremont asked.

"No, of course not. It'll be nice to have company. It gets a little lonesome out here."

"I'll try not to get in your way. Maybe we could teach each other something new about cooking."

"I'll start with these," Jeff said. He held up the string of fish. "I'll clean these if somebody will cook them."

"I'll do that," Eileen Fremont said. "Do you have any cornmeal?"

"Yes, of course, we do. I'll make some hush puppies," Leah said quickly.

While Colonel Majors played with his daughter on the floor, Eileen and Leah did the cooking. The table was soon set with a huge platter of fried fish, hush puppies, fried potatoes, turnip greens, and purple-hulled peas, and supper turned out to be a huge success.

As Colonel Majors sat down and looked at it all, his eyes grew wide. "I wish every soldier in the Army of the Confederacy had a supper like this!" he exclaimed.

He asked the blessing quickly, and Jeff grinned at him. "You sure did that in a hurry, Pa. I was afraid you was gonna say one of your long prayers."

"I'll reserve that for another time." His father winked at him.

They began to eat, and Jeff said, "These fish are cooked real good, Mrs. Fremont."

"I guess frying fish is something people from Louisiana know how to do. I grew up on a bayou," she said. "I believe I could fish before I could walk very well."

"Did you ever see an alligator in the bayou?" Leah asked.

"Yes, lots of times. They're good too."

"You mean—" Jeff stared at her "—good to *eat?*"

"Why, yes! Haven't you eaten alligator?"

"No, ma'am!" Jeff said. "I'd just as soon eat a snake."

"Well, they're not bad either. But on the whole, I'd rather have alligator than snake."

Colonel Majors was looking at his new house-keeper with amusement in his eyes. "I'd like to try that sometime."

"You'll have to come down to Louisiana after the war. I'll show you some cooking like you've never tasted."

"I'd like that."

For a while they talked about Louisiana and the Cajun people who lived there, but at last the colonel said, "Well, we better go back to camp. Will you be all right alone one more night, Leah? I'll see that Mrs. Fremont gets back tomorrow after we pick up her things."

"Oh, yes, I'll be fine."

"Better go hitch up the team, Jeff. We need to get back."

Leah followed Jeff outside. As he was finishing harnessing the horses, she drifted over to him and said rather shyly, "I hope you liked the supper, Jeff."

"It was great." He grinned at her. "Best meal I've had in a long time."

Leah wanted to say her apologies, but just as she opened her mouth, Colonel Majors and Mrs. Fremont came out of the house.

Mrs. Fremont was holding Esther, who had gone to sleep. "Would you take her, Leah?"

"Of course." Leah took the sleeping child, and the moment for apologizing to Jeff passed.

After the good-byes were said and the wagon rattled off, Leah said aloud in disgust, "Boys are pretty silly—but so are girls!"

She went back into the house, determined that the next time she saw Jeff she would tell him how sorry she was. After all, it wasn't that big a thing.

Still, she wasn't quite sure that he had Lucy Driscoll out of his mind. "I'm not jealous," she told Esther as she dressed her for bed. "It's just that Jeff and I are old friends and that Lucy's such a flirt. Boys don't know how to handle things like that. They sometimes act pretty silly."

7
Jeff Is Displeased

Eileen Fremont had taken the position of house-keeper and nurse to Colonel Majors's daughter with apprehension. Actually, she had very little choice. Louisiana had been her home, but things had been hard for her there. The Yankees occupied Baton Rouge relatively early in the war. Eileen had been willing to bear it as long as her husband was alive, but when she lost him and then in a short time her only child, the city itself seemed hateful to her. It had been almost with relief that she had undertaken the journey to Richmond to see what she could do to help her brother-in-law.

She had at first wondered if she could bear to be around another child so near the age of the daughter she had lost, but there had been an almost instant bond. Esther, she discovered, was an affectionate child and just as bright as her own had been. And at first Eileen determined not to become attached to the girl, but that had been almost impossible—perhaps because she herself was so lonely and there was a vacuum in her heart. In any case, she found herself loving the blonde little girl more and more.

Leah came into the parlor early one morning to find Eileen holding Esther in her lap. The child had fallen asleep.

"She's not sick, is she, Eileen?"

"No, I think she just had a bad dream."

"How long have you been up holding her like that?"

"Oh, I don't know. Two hours, more or less."

"Well, you should've put her back to bed," Leah admonished the older woman. "Here, let me take her."

"No, that's all right. I'll hold her."

Leah had started forward, but now she stopped and scrutinized the pair. Taking a seat on the couch across the room, she said, "You've really fallen in love with little Esther, haven't you?"

"Who could help that?" Eileen smiled. She carefully smoothed the blonde curls away from the sleeping child's forehead. "She's as sweet as my own child was."

"What was your baby's name, Eileen?"

"Juliet."

"What a lovely name! Did you pick it out?"

"No, my husband chose it. He always said we were like Romeo and Juliet, so young when we fell in love. He named her that, and I thought it was sweet." Eileen had never mentioned her husband to Leah before.

Leah hesitated. "You got married very early, didn't you?"

"I was only seventeen, and he was eighteen."

Leah's eyes grew round. "I'm almost that old myself!"

"It doesn't work well for everyone to get married at that early an age," Eileen said. "Most need to wait longer."

Leah got up and went over to look out the window. "The sun's coming up, and the cows are coming up to the barn," she commented. Then, turning around, she said, "Did you think about getting married when you were a girl?"

"Why, of course. Every girl thinks about that when she starts getting a little older. I expect you've thought about it."

"Yes, I have, but—" Leah broke off and hurriedly left the room.

Startled by her sudden departure, Eileen thought for a moment, then carefully got up. She placed the sleeping child on the sofa, threw a coverlet over her, and went into the kitchen, where she found Leah sitting at the table. "What's the matter, Leah?"

"Oh, nothing!" Leah twirled a lock of hair around her finger restlessly, then blurted out, "Did you ever have a fight with your husband—before you were married, I mean?"

At once Eileen knew exactly why Leah was troubled. "Of course," she said. "I expect sweethearts always have arguments."

"I hate them!" Leah said.

Eileen knew that Leah's mother was far away. Perhaps the girl had been keeping her thoughts to herself for so long that she desperately longed to share them with someone.

"You see, when I came back with Tom and Esther, I saw . . . my friend with this other girl—Lucy Driscoll."

Something about the way Leah pronounced the name caught Eileen's attention. "I take it you don't like Lucy very much?"

"Well, she's small and pretty. Not a big cow like I am. I'm a giantess, practically."

"Oh, I don't think that's true! You're going to be tall and stately. I think that's very attractive in a woman. I was always too short, I thought. Every time I saw a tall girl," Eileen said, "I wished I could be like her. I actually thought about stretching myself. Tying a rope around my arms and putting weights on my legs."

Leah stared at her, then giggled. "I used to think about trying to shrink myself, but I could never figure out how to do it."

"Actually, I think God knew what was best for each of us," Eileen said. "Just as He knows what's best for everyone. Now, tell me more about Lucy and Jeff."

Leah gaped at her. "How did you know I was talking about Jeff?"

"Oh, I saw the way you were looking at him and the way he was looking at you when he came to visit. You've been friends a long time, haven't you?"

"All of our lives. We did everything together when we were kids." She began talking with enthusiasm about how she and Jeff had grown up together. "But it's different now," she ended almost sullenly. "Ever since we came to Richmond, he's been paying a lot of attention to Lucy Driscoll. Her father is rich, and she has all kinds of pretty clothes. She knows how to do all the latest dances. And look at me. Why shouldn't Jeff go to the minstrel show with her? I don't blame him a bit!"

Guardedly, Eileen tried to explain how difficult it is to grow up. "All of us have to do it. Boys, too. We have to learn how to stop being children and become adults. And sometimes when we're halfway between, not quite grown, not quite a child, it's hard to know how to behave."

"Did you feel that way when you were growing up?"

Eileen laughed, her eyes sparkled, and she shook

her head in despair. "I thought I'd go crazy for a while there when I was about your age. I couldn't seem to do anything right." Eileen knew she was good at giving counsel without seeming to. She went on making light of her own foolishness and finally she saw that Leah was becoming quieter. And then Eileen said, "I even feel a little bit funny about Jeff's father."

"About Colonel Majors? Why?"

"Well, there's an officers' ball coming up, and he's asked me to go to it. I'm all confused about it."

"Why, it would be fun!"

"I suppose, but you see, all the other ladies will have nice dresses and shoes. And I don't have anything like that here."

Instantly Leah got to her feet. "Well, you *will* have, Eileen! You've got to go! We'll fix you a dress. As a matter of fact, some of my sister Sarah's dresses are still here from when we were in Richmond before. We'll fix you something that will make you the belle of the ball!"

Eileen Fremont sat quietly, amused at the girl's enthusiasm. Then, "I haven't been to a ball in I don't know when," she said. "The last time I went, it was with my husband, just before Shiloh. I think it might make me sad to go."

Leah came close and put a hand on her arm. "I think you ought to go," she said softly. "It would be good for you. Come, let's go look. Maybe one of Sarah's dresses can be taken up for you a little bit. You're smaller than she is. We've got everything we need here."

"But what about shoes?"

"We'll paint your feet black!" Leah laughed. "No,

come on. Shoes aren't important. It's going to be such fun. When is the ball?"

"On the twelfth. That's day after tomorrow!"

"Oh, that's plenty of time! You send word that you'll go, and we'll have you ready like Cinderella when Colonel Majors comes to get you."

Jeff learned about the ball on the morning of the twelfth. He came into the tent to find the colonel getting his hair cut by the regimental barber, and Jeff stood quietly watching. After the barber had left, his father said, "I'm going out to buy a new uniform—if I can find anything."

"You mean to wear when we leave?"

"No, I mean to wear tonight. I'm taking Eileen to the ball."

"You're taking Mrs. Fremont to a *ball*? But she's a servant!"

Colonel Majors was studying himself in the mirror. "Oh, I hardly think that's the case. She's just helping us out, Jeff, and she's been a *great* help. Esther's crazy about her!"

For some reason Jeff found the idea of his father taking Eileen Fremont to the ball unpleasant. He did not know how to express this, so he said nothing. But when the colonel left to go to town to search for a new uniform, Jeff went out to Uncle Silas's.

He found Leah very excited. The entire house seemed to be rather in a mess, and there was a lot of activity. "What's going on?" he asked.

Actually, Leah looked happier than he had seen her in a long time. Her eyes were shining. "I'm getting Eileen ready to go to the ball! Isn't it nice, Jeff, that she and your father are going to go together?"

74

Jeff bit his lip. "I don't think he ought to do it!"

Leah blinked and asked, "Why not?"

"Well, I don't *know* why not! It just doesn't seem right to me, that's all!"

"Not right? It'll be good for both of them. Your father hasn't had a lot of fun, you know, since he's been here in Richmond. He's been fighting, and wounded, and trying to take care of you and Tom, and worried about Esther. I think it's fine for them to go."

"Well, *that* wouldn't be too bad, but—" Jeff broke off as Eileen came into the room, wearing a robe.

"Oh, I didn't know you were here, Jeff."

"I just stopped by for a minute," Jeff said dully. "I didn't mean to interrupt."

"You couldn't do that. Why don't you go play with Esther?"

"Where is she?"

"In the bedroom. I'll get her for you." Eileen hurried off and soon returned with the little girl. "There, you two can play while I go try to do something with my hair."

"I'll help you with it if you need me, Eileen," Leah called after her. She turned to Jeff and asked quietly, so that Mrs. Fremont couldn't hear, "What is wrong with you, Jeff? Don't you like Eileen?"

Jeff picked up Esther. "I don't know why you call her Eileen. She's a grown woman. You ought to call her Mrs. Fremont."

"She *told* me to call her Eileen. It would be real odd calling her Mrs. Fremont when we're together all the time. Don't you *like* her, Jeff?" she repeated. "I think she's wonderful!"

"She's all right, I guess," Jeff said reluctantly. There was a pouting look on his face. He took Esther and plumped down on the sofa. He'd had mixed feelings from the very beginning about Eileen Fremont, and now he wished that he had not come to the house. He half rose, saying, "I guess I better get back . . ."

"You sit right down there, Jeff Majors, and tell me what's the matter with you! You're pouting like a mule that's been eating briars!"

Jeff glared. "You're the one that knows how to pout. You've been swelled up like a dead possum ever since you saw me with Lucy at the minstrel show!"

Leah sat beside him and looked him right in the eye. "Jeff, I was wrong about that. I'm sorry that I acted so badly. Do you forgive me?"

Her apology took the wind out of Jeff's sails. Flustered, he let Esther scoot down to the floor. "Well . . . well, sure I will," he said. "But why did you get so mad anyway? It was just a trip to a minstrel show."

"Yes, but I saw her kiss you."

Jeff flushed to the roots of his hair. "Oh, shoot!" he said explosively. "You know how Lucy is! She's always kissing somebody! I'd just told her I was gonna ask Pa to let her come to the Regimental Band Concert, and she got all excited about it. A kiss doesn't mean anything with Lucy."

"I know. That's just her way. I'm just silly, Jeff. I don't see how you've put up with me all these years."

Jeff felt rather strange. For days now, Leah had been angry and upset with him, and now all of a sudden, just as if she had thrown a switch, she was apologetic. He saw that she really meant it too, and he quickly said, "Oh, that's all right. I guess I've been pretty silly myself a time or two."

"That's sweet of you, Jeff. Most boys wouldn't be so honest."

This flustered him even more. "I don't know if I'm all that honest," he said. He glanced about the room. "I can't tell you how I feel about Mrs. Fremont." He refused to call her Eileen. "I'm worried about Pa."

"You mean that he might get hurt in the battle?"

"There's always that. We never quite put that out of our minds, I guess, but it's more than that. You know, I've been studying people a long time, and I've noticed something about men."

"What, Jeff?"

"I've noticed that every time a man loses his wife, sooner or later he gets anxious to get married again."

Leah stared at him. "Well, that's natural. Especially for a young man like your father. Why, he *needs* a wife. I know you miss your mother and respect her, but—"

"It's not just that. I've seen some men go off and marry the wrong women. You remember when Sam Doogle's wife died back in Pineville? She was a good woman, Heddy was. Steady and good with the kids. So what did Sam do?"

"He married Joyce Reynolds."

"Yeah, and you know what Joyce Reynolds was. She was no good from the start. She hadn't been married to Sam for a month before she started fluttering her eyelashes at other men. You know what a mess that was."

"That doesn't have anything to do with this, Jeff. Eileen's not like that."

77

"How do you know?" Jeff demanded. "You've only been around her a few days. You don't know what she's like."

"I know she's very sweet and gentle—"

"And she's got a temper like a buzz saw. Pa said that his own self!" Jeff exclaimed. "Why, the first time she come into that tent, Pa said she raked him up one side and down the other! Now, what's it going to be like if he marries a woman like that, always losing her temper?"

"I don't know anything about that! I haven't seen her lose her temper."

"Well, she did! You just ask Tom! He heard it!"

"I don't think you can judge a person that easily, Jeff. All of us lose our temper sometimes. Why, suppose a stranger had seen *me* the last few days, all angry and sullen. But I'm not like that all the time."

"I reckon that's right enough, but everything's in a rush because of this blasted war. I just don't think Pa ought to go to that ball with her, that's all!"

For a long time Leah tried to talk to Jeff. She said she was amazed that he was so stubborn.

And then he blurted out, "She's just not like Ma! That's all there is to it!"

"Nobody is exactly like your mother, Jeff. Nobody ever could be. God made each one of us like we are. Think what a world it would be if everyone were just like you."

"What's wrong with me?" Jeff demanded. "Nothing!"

"Nothing, but if everybody were just like you, it would be awfully boring, for one thing. God made us all different and for a purpose. The preacher said that last Sunday. Don't you remember?"

"Well, Mrs. Fremont is too different from Ma. Ma was quiet and real gentle, and Mrs. Fremont is redheaded and hot-tempered. She goes charging around like she's got a full head of steam all the time."

"I think that's a very attractive way. It's natural with her. And she's very lonely, Jeff. She lost her husband and baby. She needs a husband, and she's so in love with Esther. It makes you almost cry to see it."

"Well, it doesn't make me cry!" Jeff announced. He stood up, his back ramrod straight. "I'm going back to camp!" He marched to the door but turned around before going out. "I'm right glad we made up, Leah. I sure don't like to fuss with you."

"I'm glad too, Jeff." If Leah wanted to say another word about Eileen, the still-stubborn look in Jeff's eyes must have kept her from it. "Why don't you come back and stay with Esther and me while your father is at the ball?"

Jeff hesitated, then nodded. "Well . . . I reckon I might do that."

"If you don't have to go back," she said quickly, "you could stay right now."

Jeff considered that. "Pa said I might want to do that, and I told him I probably wouldn't."

"Come on, Jeff. I'll tell you what. We'll make popcorn balls. You always like to do that."

Enticed by the promise of popcorn balls, which he loved, Jeff said, "Well, I guess it'd be all right. We could take Esther down to the creek, and she can watch me catch fish again."

"All right, Jeff."

Leah ran at once to tell Eileen. "Jeff's going to stay with me while you and his father go to the ball. We're going to make popcorn balls."

Eileen smiled. "I think I'm doing the wrong thing, but you talked me into it."

"You're doing the *right* thing! Now, you go to that ball, and you have the best time you ever had in your whole life!"

8
At the Ball

Jeff did not eat much supper, Leah noticed, at least not as much as he usually did. That is to say, he ate only two whole baked potatoes, a huge chunk of smoked ham, a medium-sized bowl of butter beans, and four biscuits.

She smiled sweetly and said, "Well, Jeff, I guess you're too full to eat anything else."

He leaned back and patted his stomach. "Sure am. You did a good job, Leah."

"I guess I'll have to save the apple pie for somebody else."

Jeff's eyes flew open. "You've got apple pie? Why didn't you tell me?"

"I *am* telling you. I'll just have a piece for me, and you could have some, couldn't you, Eileen?"

Eileen seemed amused by the scene between the two young people. She'd mentioned to Leah that Jeff was rather stiff in his behavior toward her, and that she regretted it for she found him a very handsome and attractive young man—much like his father. "I believe I could have a small piece," she said demurely.

When Leah got up to get the pie, Eileen reached across and gave Esther a spoonful of peas. "Chew them good," she said.

"Chew! Peas good!" Esther crowed.

"She certainly is a beautiful child, Jeff. And Leah

tells me she looks exactly like your mother with her blonde hair and blue eyes."

"I guess so," Jeff grunted, not looking up.

Leah noticed his behavior and slammed down his pie in front of him with more force than was necessary. She was upset with Jeff because he persisted in his mulish behavior. "Well, there it is."

Jeff glanced at her and then quickly back down at the pie. Picking up his fork, he sliced off a healthy wedge, speared it, then put it in his mouth. "Good," he mumbled around the huge mouthful. But when he took a sip of coffee made from acorns, he made a face. "I wish the coffee was as good as the pie!"

"If the war doesn't end pretty soon, some people will forget what real coffee tastes like," Leah said.

"Guess so," Jeff muttered.

"Come along, Eileen, it's time to get you ready," Leah said. "Jeff, you can wash the dishes. And look after Esther."

Jeff waited until the two women had left the room, then said under his breath, "Glad to, Leah, now that you have asked me so politely."

He looked over at Esther, who was grinning at him. He walked around the table, sat beside her, and wiped her face with a damp cloth. "I wish everybody was as sweet and pretty as you are, Esther," he whispered. "It would be a mighty good world." Then he put her on the floor, where she played around his feet and generally got in the way as he washed the dishes in the sink.

When he'd finished that chore, he wandered into the sitting room, with Esther padding along beside him. Sitting on the floor, he got out some of her toys and played with her until he heard the sound of a horse and carriage outside.

"That must be Pa," he said. He got to his feet, and when a knock came at the door, he was there to answer it. "Come on in, Pa. I mean, Colonel."

"I guess it can be Pa tonight," Nelson Majors said. "How do you like the new uniform? Absolutely the last one in all Richmond." He turned around to give Jeff a good look. The uniform he wore was ash-gray, and he had a scarlet sash around his waist. The coat was long, and its brass buttons gleamed in the lamplight. His boots glowed with a bright burnish. The hat he held by his side had a small, black, feathered plume in it.

"Wow, Pa," Jeff said almost reverently. "You look great. If you drop dead, we won't have to do a thing to you."

"Jeff, you have a way of phrasing things that . . . well . . . well, thanks anyway for the compliment, if that's what it was."

"It was, Pa. You look great! Come on in and let Esther take a look at you in all your glory."

In the sitting room, Esther ran to him instantly.

The colonel picked her up, tossed her into the air, listened to her squeal, then sat down with her on his lap. "Tell me what you've been doing," he said and listened as, in her babyish prattle, she told of her adventures of the day. After a time he turned to Jeff. "She seems to be happy with her new nurse."

"I guess so," Jeff said uncomfortably. He had not said anything to his father about his displeasure, and he was glad he had not.

At that moment, he heard steps coming down the hallway, and both men looked toward the door.

Leah stepped inside, a smile on her face. "And now, I give you the queen of the ball, Mrs. Eileen Fremont!"

She waved her hand, and Eileen came into the room, her cheeks rosy. "What a lot of nonsense," she said. "Hello, Colonel."

Nelson stared at her. She was wearing a bright yellow evening gown with a deep-pointed bodice. The short sleeves were hidden under epaulettes of lace and trimmed with small, light pink silk flowers. The overskirt was gathered at the waist and very full, reaching to just above the knees, while the skirt underneath almost touched the floor and was decorated with small lace flounces and more silk flowers. Her hair was brushed back off her face, leaving a few small ringlets at each side, and was ornamented with pale pink flowers. She had on white elbow-length gloves.

"You look lovely, Eileen," Colonel Majors said.

"Well, if I'm presentable, it's because Leah's such a good dressmaker. Actually, you've seen this dress before."

"I have?"

"Yes, it belongs to Sarah," Leah said. "Don't you remember? She wore it to a ball once."

"I guess I'd forgotten. Anyway, you look fine." He pulled his watch out of his inner pocket and glanced at it. "And I guess we'd better get going if we want to be there for the opening promenade."

As Eileen joined him at the door, the colonel said, "We may be back late, Jeff. I take it you're staying. You can ride back to camp with me, of course."

"All right, Pa." Jeff waited until the door closed, then shook his head. "I never seen Pa act like that.

Why, you'd think he was eighteen years old and was going to his first party."

"I think your father gets lonesome, Jeff. When a man has a wife, he has company. Your father's been alone now for three years."

"Well, anyway, I don't expect she'll stay too long. She'll probably go back to Baton Rouge soon."

If Leah suspected that Eileen had no such idea, she did not choose to let Jeff know this. "Let's pop the popcorn," she said, "and then we'll make balls. Come on, Esther—I'll give you your first lesson on how to pop corn."

Eileen Fremont had not been to a party since before the Battle of Shiloh early in the war. As she moved around the ballroom floor to a waltz, she was very conscious of this. Somehow she felt vaguely guilty about coming and said so.

"I really shouldn't be doing this, Colonel."

Nelson Majors looked down at her. "Why in the world not? It's innocent enough. There won't be many more balls like this in the Confederacy, I think."

"I don't know why. I just sometimes think that I'm still married, even though my husband has been dead for two years."

He maneuvered her in a sweeping curve and looked out over the ballroom. The women's red, yellow, green, and blue dresses made a colorful sight amid the officers' gray uniforms, glittering brass buttons, and polished black boots. He listened to the band playing, then said, "I know. I feel the same way. I suppose when you're married to someone that you love, you think it can never end. But it does."

"Well," she said brightly, apparently trying to lighten the conversation, "I've danced three dances straight with you. Are we going to have every dance?"

"No, the general over there has warned me he'll have me court-martialed if he doesn't get the next one."

"Oh, we mustn't let that happen! But right now, tell me some more about what you did in Kentucky."

When the ball ended, Nelson was shocked at how late it was. He said so as he helped Eileen into the carriage. "Why, it's after one o'clock. We won't get you back to the house until one thirty!"

"Everybody may be asleep," she said. She waited until he got inside and picked up the lines, and then, as the carriage moved off, began talking about the officers of the regiment. "They all seem very young."

"Most of the older ones haven't made it this far," Nelson said. He quickly amended his statement. "I didn't mean to say that."

"It's all right, Colonel."

Nelson looked at her and said, "Look, when you call me colonel I feel as old as Methuselah. You think you could use my name for the rest of the evening?"

"Of course, Nelson, if you think it's proper for a housekeeper to address the master by his first name."

They passed a street lamp, and the light fell across her face. He had never seen a woman more calm, which surprised him. "When you first came storming into my office," he said, "I thought you had a temper like musket fire, but you don't, really."

"Yes, I do—when things go wrong. I like to have my own way." She smiled at him, and he smiled back. "I suppose most of us want our own way, but few of us get it."

They chatted amiably as the horse plodded on down the road. He talked mostly of Kentucky and his life there. "I had a nice farm, and it was good. I had to sell it when we came to Richmond."

"You never know. Maybe you can go back there when the war's over."

"I wouldn't be very welcome, I'm afraid," he said soberly. "Most of the people in that area are for the Union. They wouldn't want a Rebel back in the midst of them. I'd like to go back, though. And Jeff and Tom loved it there."

When they got to the house and Nelson pulled up the horse, he said, "Great guns! I've never talked so much in my whole life. I've bored you to death, Eileen."

"I haven't been bored." Her voice was quiet.

They sat listening as an owl crossed the sky, making a lonely cry.

"It's a beautiful evening," she said. "I love the full moon." She looked up at the huge, silver disk and added, "Look, you can even see the pockmarks on it!" She turned to him. "I used to look to see the man in the moon, but I never saw him."

"Neither did I! He'd be a pretty old fellow by this time, I think." Nelson admired the stars that dotted the heavens and said, "I wish I knew the names of all those. The Bible says God calls them all by name."

"That's a nice thought—that He named all the stars."

"I find a lot of comfort in the Bible," he said. "I miss my church back in Kentucky, although we've had some good chaplains. There's just something about taking your family and going into a church, sitting down, looking at people, listening to the sermon, singing together. I miss that a lot."

"I'm sure you do. I love church too."

The two sat in the buggy talking until finally Eileen said, "Well, it's very late . . ."

"Of course it is." He wrapped the lines tightly, jumped out, then walked around to her side and helped her to the ground. They stood facing each other. "I can't tell you what this has meant to me, Eileen. I've been, to tell the truth, a little bit lonely."

"I guess we've both been lonely. It's been nice for me too."

He did not want the moment to end. He took her hand. "I guess I'll never know how to thank you for the way you've come to take care of Esther for me." He bent over and kissed her hand and smiled. "Thank you very much, Mrs. Fremont."

"You're very welcome, Nelson. And I . . . I wish you didn't have to go into battle."

Something in her voice touched the colonel. Without planning to, he took her in his arms and kissed her. When he stepped back, he said, "I can't apologize for that."

"I don't think you have to."

Inside the house, Jeff peered through the front window. He saw his father kiss Eileen Fremont, and at once he straightened up.

Leah, standing at his side, touched his arm. She understood. "Don't let it bother you, Jeff."

He did not answer, however, and when the colonel and Eileen came in and his father said, "Well, *we* had a great time. How about you folks?" Jeff said nothing.

Leah spoke up quickly. "Oh, we had a good time here too. We made popcorn balls for you to take back to some of the officers."

"That'll be fine, Leah. Thank you. Well, let's get back to camp, Jeff. Thanks again for the lovely evening, Eileen."

"It was a pleasure, Colonel."

As soon as the two men left, Eileen turned to Leah. "Jeff was angry, wasn't he?"

"He saw his father kiss you. I think he's very upset."

"That often happens when young people lose their mothers. They're bound to feel some resentment toward anyone who tries to take their place. I'm sorry for it."

"He'll be all right. Jeff gets like that sometimes." Leah hesitated, then said, "I get that way myself. Sort of bullheaded." She put her arms around the older woman. "Now, come along. I want to hear all about the ball . . ."

9
Smoke in the Wilderness

On the morning the troops departed, Leah rose early and found that Eileen was already up and preparing to go to town.

"I didn't know you were going to see the men off, Eileen," she said, rubbing the sleep from her eyes.

Eileen was fixing breakfast, and Esther was clinging to her skirts, babbling as usual. Finally Eileen stooped down, picked the child up, and kissed her. "You go play. I can't work with you pulling at me like that." She gave the child a gentle shove and watched as Esther ran off. Then she turned to Leah. "It's a sad day. Nelson told me yesterday that they'd be pulling out early, and I want to be there to see him off."

Leah took some plates out of the cabinet and set the table. "It is sad, isn't it? It's just awful to watch men leave and know that some of them will come back crippled and some of them . . . won't come back at all."

A shiver seemed to go over Eileen. "I went through this before. A long time ago, it seems now. I remember when John—my husband—went away. We thought he'd be back in a few weeks. The flags were flying, and the bands were playing, and it was very exciting down in Baton Rouge. But he never came back."

Silence fell over the kitchen as the two were preoccupied with their own thoughts. Finally Eileen shook her shoulders. "Well, we can't let the men see us sad like this. Women have to be cheerful, no matter what."

It made Leah feel good that Eileen referred to her as a woman, not as a little girl. "That's right," she said. "I'll go get Esther. Then, after breakfast, I'll hitch up the team to the buggy. What are you going to wear?"

"The best dress I have." Eileen smiled. "And so must you. We want to give Jeff something to remember you by."

"And give his father the same thing, Eileen." And Leah went off to get Esther.

To Leah it seemed that every soul in Richmond and the surrounding countryside had come to see the troops off. The town square was full. The streets were packed, and from somewhere a band played "Dixie." There were not as many people as when the men had first gone off to war, back before Bull Run. Still, there was a desperate attempt at gaiety.

She found Jeff at the end of the main street, helping get the men together to form a parade. She had decided to wear a light blue-green dress that matched her eyes, and Jeff seemed to think she looked very pretty. He smiled and said so as she came up. "Well, aren't you dressed up."

"Hello, Jeff. We had to come in and see you off. Where's your father?"

"There he is—right over there—trying to get everything ready. It's like getting ready to go on a long trip. You're sure to forget something. We just don't know yet what it is."

"Is Tom going along?"

"Yes. Pa didn't want him to, but he just insisted on it. Said he could at least take notes and polish Pa's boots. I wouldn't be surprised, though, if he didn't pick up a musket and get in the thick of it. You know Tom."

Jeff's lighthearted reference to battle saddened Leah, but she tried not to show it. "I want to say good-bye to the rest of your squad."

She had become well acquainted with the members of the squad of which Jeff was a part. When she found the boys, she went around and talked to them one at a time.

First she went up to Charlie Bowers, the same age as Jeff and also still a drummer boy. "You be careful, Charlie. Just play the drums and don't get in any trouble," she said, shaking his hand.

Charlie grinned at her. "Don't you worry, Miss Leah." He looked over at Jeff, then back at Leah. "And I'll take care of your sweetie pie there."

Leah blushed and turned quickly to Curly Henson, the big redheaded soldier who had saved Jeff's life at Bull Run. "Good-bye, Curly."

"Good-bye, Miss Leah. We'll be comin' right back with them Yankee scalps on our belt."

Sgt. Henry Mapes, a tall, rangy man with black eyes and hair, grinned at Henson. "I ain't noticed you winnin' any medals, Curly." Then he turned to Leah. "We sure thank you for them cookies and cakes you been sendin', Miss Leah."

"I brought a whole big box of cookies and candy today. I'll give it to you to guard, Sergeant."

As Leah went on down the line, shaking hands with all of the young soldiers, the thought came to her, *Some of them are not much older than Jeff. By next year he'll be in the regular army!*

"This is a new volunteer, Leah," Jeff said, nodding toward an undersized soldier with blond hair and pale blue eyes. "This is Ocie Landers. He comes from Mississippi. Just joined up with the Stonewall Brigade."

"I'm glad to know you, Ocie." Seeing that the boy was bashful, Leah put out her hand first. He took it and released it very quickly. Somehow Leah knew he was afraid. "You know, I baked a special batch of taffy, Ocie, and I want you to be sure to have some of it. Why don't you come along with me, and I'll give it to you right now?"

Ocie looked confused, but Jeff winked at him. "You better take her up on that, Ocie. It's going to be a long time before you get any candy as good as Leah makes."

For the next twenty minutes Leah talked to Ocie. She found that he was very homesick, that he missed his girlfriend back home, and that he was indeed afraid.

He said, "I didn't want to tell any of the fellas, but I'm just about scared to death. I wouldn't want them to know it," he added quickly.

"They're all afraid too, Ocie. You don't have to be ashamed of that."

Ocie stared at her. *"They're* not afraid. Not Jeff."

"You ask him," Leah said. "They've been in battle before, and they've learned how to kind of cover it up, but I think every man that goes into battle is afraid."

This seemed to encourage Ocie, and he brightened. As they walked back toward Jeff, he said, "I'll never forget you giving me this candy."

Leah said, "You just trust the Lord, and He'll take care of you, whatever happens."

"Well, I'm doin' that," Ocie said quickly. "I got saved in a revival meeting back home—just last summer. It was out in a brush arbor."

"I'm glad to hear that." Leah smiled, shook hands with him again, and then went back to Jeff. As they walked along the line of soldiers preparing to board the train, she said, "Jeff, be careful about Ocie. He's afraid, but he doesn't want anybody to know it."

"Well, he's not the only one," he said. "Not right now with the flags flying and the bands playing, but the closer we get to battle, the tighter I get on the inside. Never changes, it seems like." They glanced back at Ocie—he looked very small, watching them as they walked away. "He's just about like I was before Bull Run." Jeff looked then at Leah. "But you did a lot of good with him. And I'll stick close to him."

Back at the head of the line, Jeff looked around for his father. Tom was standing there with a roster sheet in his hand. "Where's the colonel?" Jeff asked, remembering for once not to call him "Pa."

"Oh, him and Miss Eileen went to do somethin'. I don't know what," Tom said. When Jeff turned around, Tom winked at Leah.

She smiled, knowing that there was something special about this farewell for the boys' father.

The train loosed a screaming blast, and an exhaust of steam burst from the engine. The engineer waved at Tom, calling, "All right, get aboard. You sergeants be sure all your men are on the train."

Tom reached over suddenly and gave Leah a big hug and a kiss on the cheek. "I'll be thinking about you, Leah." He hesitated, then said, "If I have bad luck, tell Sarah I loved her, will you?"

"I'll tell her, Tom."

Then Leah turned to Jeff, who stood uncertainly before her. She didn't know what to say to him. Then she put out her hand and said, "Well, Jeff, I'll be seeing you soon."

Jeff also seemed uncertain. She knew he hated good-byes, especially good-byes like this. "Sure," he said, "I hope so. You take good care of Esther, but then I know you will."

"Eileen and I will give her the best care we can."

At that moment Eileen and Colonel Majors came around the corner of the station. Leah saw that Eileen's face was flushed, and she looked more flustered than Leah had ever seen her.

When the two came up, Jeff put his hand out and said, "Good-bye, Mrs. Fremont."

But Eileen Fremont ignored his hand. She put her arms around him, pulled his head down, and kissed him on the cheek. "Good-bye, Jeff. You take care of your father."

"Sure," Jeff said, "I'll do that." He turned away from Eileen—and bumped into Leah.

To his obvious shock, she put her arms around him and kissed him on the other cheek. "That makes it a balanced set." Then she laughed at his confusion.

The men all piled onto the train, and soon Jeff was leaning out a window, along with Tom and his father. They waved as the engineer gave another blast of the whistle, and then with a clank and a jerk the cars began to move. The crowd standing at the station blurred as the train picked up speed, and then they were gone.

The three men returned to their seats, and somehow Jeff felt drained and empty.

"Sure is hard to say good-bye," Nelson Majors said. His face was grave, but then a smile came. "But it's a little better knowing that Eileen's there to take care of Esther."

Jeff looked at his father's face. He almost said, "Yeah, that's right, Pa." But he still had some stubbornness in him and, instead, just sat quietly and watched the countryside flash by.

The battle that came to be known as the Battle of the Wilderness was one of the most awesome and bitter campaigns in the Civil War. Four armies were involved—two Union armies and two Confederate forces made up of Lee's Army of Northern Virginia and the army that had been hastily gathered in Richmond.

Jeff would alight from the train one day and on the next day hear the guns begin to sound. He overheard his father tell an officer on his staff, "I figure we've got around sixty-two thousand men, and it looks like the Yankees have about a hundred and ten thousand. We're in for it this time."

Quickly the troops were rushed into position.

That night General Grant started his army marching, hoping he could get through the Wilderness without having to fight there. The Wilderness was a tangled mass of undergrowth, saplings, hills, creeks. It was impossible to march an army across in order. The roads were winding, and just dragging their guns took all the strength that the Union troops could muster.

Gen. Robert E. Lee had not been caught off guard. Somehow, with that military genius that belonged to him, he knew exactly what Grant would do, and he placed his smaller army directly in the Federals' path.

When Lee called his staff officers together, he said, "There will not be large troop movements in this battle. It will be man against man, squad against squad. I can give you no orders except to say, if we do not stop the Union army at this point, the war will be over."

It was Jeff's job as drummer boy to sound calls to the waiting troops. They would hear the drummed orders and perform maneuvers—right, left, forward, charge, retreat. But here in such undergrowth, there really were no companies or battalions—just a mass of men. Jeff's part in this battle would be very small.

He said to Tom—who had insisted on coming into the line—"Shucks, Tom! There's no sense of having a drummer boy here. I'm gonna get me a musket first chance I get."

Tom stared at his brother. "Pa will have your head if he sees you doin' it."

"I don't think he's gonna see much. You can't see more than ten yards in this blasted woods." He peered through the thick underbrush. "We've never fought in a mess like this before."

"The Yankees haven't either," Tom said grimly, no doubt purposing in his own mind to do exactly as Jeff had suggested—get a musket and be what help he could.

Jeff moved away from Tom, the drum hanging from his waist. It felt like so much dead weight.

As he reached the end of the line, he suddenly found himself face to face with Chaplain Phineas Rollins. Chaplain Rollins was tall and rawboned and wore a perpetual smile. He had known Jeff for a long time and greeted him cheerfully. "Well, it looks like a big one, Jeff," he said.

"Sure does, Chaplain. You better get yourself back a ways. Stay at the back of the fight."

Rollins looked around. He had been a soldier himself in his younger days. "I don't think there is any 'back' to this fight—just the middle of the woods with men shooting."

Then the chaplain noticed a young man who was watching them with interest. "Hello, Private. I'm Chaplain Rollins."

"This is Ocie Landers, Chaplain," Jeff said. "He's a new recruit."

Rollins put his big hand out, and the boy took it. "Good to see you, Ocie. Where are you from?" As he stood talking with the young soldier, the chaplain asked, "Do you know the Lord, Ocie?"

"Yes, sir. I got saved last summer."

"Well, that's good," the chaplain said. He looked around. "Some of these other fellows aren't saved. You might help me to tell 'em about the Lord Jesus."

Ocie said, "I ain't no preacher, Chaplain."

"You don't have to be a preacher to tell somebody that you're saved." He clapped the boy on the back, and the two were still talking when Jeff left.

Walking along farther, Jeff talked to other men and found that they were as nervous as he was. And then the sudden explosion of guns up ahead made him stop. It was rapid musket fire, and it sounded to Jeff, as it always did, like thousands of sticks being broken.

"Well," he said, running back to Tom, "I reckon it's going to happen. They're comin'."

"I think they are," Tom said. "Come on, let's get

us a musket. We can't fight 'em with a muster book and a drum."

Tom led the way to some spare weapons, and both of them picked up ammunition. Then they waited.

Finally Jeff, who had very sharp eyes, said, "I see the flash of guns up there. They're comin' this way."

From that moment on, Jeff would remember very little of the Battle of the Wilderness. All morning he just fired, reloaded, and fired again. It was impossible to see anything. Once the muskets began to fire, black smoke filled the woods. Oftentimes he simply fired in the general direction of the enemy.

A lieutenant came by and led one of the companies off to the right. Jeff and Tom went along with their squad. It was then they found out that General Longstreet had been shot.

"And it was just about a year ago that General Jackson got killed—shot by his own men by accident," Jeff said. His face was black, and he was panting from the heat. He looked upward through the smoke and said, "I can't see that we're winnin' or losin'." He had passed the bodies of several Yankee soldiers, but he had also seen bodies that wore the Confederate uniform.

Late in the afternoon, Jeff saw something that made his blood run cold. "The woods are on fire! We've got to get out of here, Tom!"

"I think you're right."

Jeff and Tom began backing out, away from the flames, gathering the squad as they went. When they got to safety, Tom said, "Let's count everybody and be sure we all got out. I hope none of the fellas got hit."

Jeff waited as Tom counted, calling out the men's names. But when he called, "Landers!" there was no answer.

"Where is Ocie?" Jeff cried with alarm.

"He was right beside me back there," Charlie Bowers said.

Curly Henson shook his head. "Then I reckon he got hit."

Instantly Jeff said, "We got to go back and get him!"

"You can't go back in there!" Tom said. "Not with the woods on fire!"

Jeff could not help but think of the boy who was perhaps dead but also perhaps alive. *If he's alive and can't move,* Jeff thought, *he'll be burned up!*

He said no more to any of the squad but quietly crept away. As soon as he was out of sight, he broke into a run. Ahead, the woods were glowing, but he ignored that. He knew that he could run into gunfire, not only from the Yankees but from Confederates who could not distinguish uniforms in the hazy air. But he kept going.

He ran down through a gully and up the hill the squad had occupied. "Ocie—Ocie, are you here?"

There was no answer, and Jeff pressed farther in. To his right a wall of fire now ate away at the dried wood and leaves and vines. The heat singed his face. He went farther on—and finally stopped in despair.

"Can't get no further," he said. He raised his voice one more time and called out, "Ocie, where are you?" He paused and thought he heard a faint voice say, "Over here!"

"Where, Ocie?" Jeff wheeled around and moved in the direction of the voice.

100

"Over here!"

He heard the voice more clearly, and then Jeff broke into a run. He saw a small form lying at the base of a huge oak. The fire was barely ten feet on the other side of him and closing in.

"Ocie, are you OK?"

"I got . . . shot in the leg."

"Let me see." Bending over, Jeff saw that his injury was not bad. It appeared to be just a flesh wound. "Can you walk?"

"Maybe I can if you help me. It hurts like fury, Jeff."

"Then, come on—put your arm around my neck." He helped the boy to his feet, and the two, their faces blistered by the raging flames, struggled back to safety.

When they were out of danger of the fire, Ocie said, "I asked Jesus to send somebody to get me, and I guess you're him, Jeff—or maybe an angel."

Jeff looked down at the smaller boy and grinned. "Well, I've been called lots of things but never an angel."

"I sure was glad to see you comin'. But there's some more of our fellas back there, I'm afraid."

The thought sobered both of them.

When they were back with the rest of the squad, Ocie said again, "I'm sure glad you came, Jeff. That was bad back there—but I knew that Jesus would send somebody."

10

A Casualty

Jeff looked around at his squad, all of them thirsty and hungry and exhausted. They had all hoped that Grant, who lost thousands of men in the Battle of the Wilderness, would turn and go back to Washington. All the other Federal commanders had done exactly this, including General McClellan.

"Grant's a different sort of general," Colonel Majors said. He had stopped by to encourage the boys. "He's not going to back up, no matter how many men he loses. We'll just have to keep on fighting."

As Ocie watched the colonel walk on, speaking to other squads, he said, "That's some pappy you got there, Jeff! He is really something!"

Jeff felt a wave of pride sweep through him but said only, "Yes, he is, isn't he?" He had always been proud of his father but never more so than now. Some officers stayed at the rear, but Colonel Majors was always at the front. As Charlie Bowers said, "All you got to do is look around, and there's the colonel right up in the front with the rest of us."

One morning the colonel came to say, "We're moving out."

"Where we going, Colonel?" a lieutenant asked wearily.

"Spotsylvania. That's where Grant will hit next. At least that's what General Lee says."

The lieutenant looked puzzled. "How in the world can General Lee *know* that?"

"General Lee's got a lot of respect for Grant," Colonel Majors said. "He said it's what he would do if he were Grant. So here we go—Spotsylvania."

Both armies moved out at night, General Grant indeed marching toward Spotsylvania. But General Lee moved his men faster, and when Grant got there he found the Confederates in place before him. During the next twelve days, Grant threw his troops again and again against the Southern positions. Union losses mounted higher and higher—much higher than those of the Confederates. The Federal forces, however, had replacements, while Lee's army was steadily growing weaker, for there were too few men left in the South to fill the ranks.

One morning, when the battle had been going on for several days, Jeff saw his father coming back to camp, his face downcast. "What's the matter?" Jeff asked.

"It's General Jeb Stuart. He's been killed in battle at a place called Yellow Tavern."

Jeb Stuart was the greatest of the great cavalry commanders—the greatest on either side, most people said. The loss of this leader saddened Jeff. He had once met General Stuart in company with his father and admired him greatly. "That's too bad. He was a great man."

Colonel Majors stood silent for a moment. Then, "They're getting us one by one," he said quietly. "There's only one end to that."

"You don't think we can win the war?" Jeff asked. This had never really seriously occurred to him.

Colonel Majors looked at Jeff, his eyes holding those of his son. "We're just not strong enough, Jeff.

We do our best, but they're just too many for us—too many men, too many guns." He turned and walked away sadly.

And there, at the Battle of Spotsylvania, Jeff Majors realized for the first time that the South was going to lose the war.

After several hard-fought battles, the armies found themselves at a place called Cold Harbor. The Confederates had retreated almost daily. Now, General Grant decided to make a supreme effort to finish the Southern army. He faced his generals and said, "We'll throw everything we have at Lee. We've got to stop this thing!"

Several of his officers tried to warn him. "General Grant, the Confederates have dug-in positions here. It will be suicide to put our men across that field."

But Grant would not be swayed. He gave the command, and thousands of Union troops rose up and marched against the Confederate position.

Jeff was standing beside the colonel in the line of riflemen, and he saw the mass of men coming. "Look at that, Pa!" he said, forgetting again to use his father's military title. "I didn't think anybody would charge across open ground against riflemen like that."

"It's a mistake," the colonel said quietly. "We made the same mistake at Gettysburg, and now it looks like it's the Union's turn."

Jeff watched the troops come on and on and on.

His father cried out, "Fire!" and a sheet of flame literally wiped out the first wave of Federal troops. It sickened Jeff to see men falling in the dust.

His father put an arm around him. "It's too bad you have to see this, Jeff."

Again and again General Grant sent his troops forward, but the Confederates held fast. The field was full of dying and wounded before he finally called an end.

"We'll have to take Richmond by siege," Grant said. "We can never attack it head-on again." Later on, after the war, he was to say, "The only thing I ever did that I regret during the whole war was to order the charge at Cold Harbor."

Jeff was on the line when the last charge was made. When he saw the Yankees driven back, he breathed, "I just hope they don't come back again."

At that moment, he heard his name called.

"What is it, Tom?"

Tom was hurrying toward him. "It's Pa. He's been shot! I've got to get him back to the hospital in Richmond."

"Not the field hospital?"

"No, they told me to take him to Chimborazo."

Chimborazo was the largest Confederate hospital. It was overcrowded but was still the best place that existed in the Confederacy for a wounded man.

"I'll go with you."

"No, you can't do that," Tom said. "You'll have to stay here with the rest of your squad. Pa said that much."

"I've got to see him!"

"Come on, then. We're taking him back right away."

Jeff followed Tom—who limped along, his artificial leg appearing to give him considerable pain—and found his father lying beside an ambulance wagon. The colonel's gray uniform was red with blood. The sight frightened Jeff, and he knelt beside him. "Pa, you're not going to die, are you?"

"No, I'm too tough a bird for that," Colonel Majors gasped. "I wish you could go with me, Jeff, but you'll have to stay. General Lee needs every man he can get, and I guess you'll have to be a man before your time."

"Sure, Pa." Jeff swallowed hard. "I wish I could go with you too, but I'll do like you say."

Carefully Jeff and Tom, assisted by the attendants, put their father in the ambulance with other wounded soldiers. Tom got into the ambulance with him, and Jeff stood at the back of the wagon. "Good-bye, Pa."

"I'll be praying for you, Jeff . . . God's going to . . . take care of both of us."

"Sure, Pa." Jeff reached into the ambulance, took his father's hand, and squeezed it hard. Then the curtains closed, the horses stepped out, and the ambulance rolled off in the direction of Richmond.

Jeff turned back to the lines, his heart filled with grief. *What will happen if Pa dies?* was the thought that was in his heart.

When the ambulance drew up in front of a low building—one of many dozens—Tom Majors got down stiffly. His leg was hurting him. He said to the driver and the helper, "I'll go inside and find a place. You get him out of the wagon and put him on a stretcher."

As he entered the hospital, he was shocked to see that it was packed with wounded. Even the halls and the entrance room had men lying alongside the walls. Some of them looked to be dead, and Tom's heart failed him as he saw there would be little hope for his father here.

He pushed his way to a desk where a man in civilian clothes was trying to give orders to a dozen people at once. They all appeared to be trying to get their people into better care.

"I've got to get my father in. He's Colonel Nelson Majors."

The small man stared at him. "Just bring him on in and put him along the wall somewhere. He'll have to take his turn."

"But he's got to be operated on. He's got a bullet in him!"

"So do all these men. Why do you think they're here?" the man snapped.

Tom wanted to say more but knew it was hopeless. He went back outside and said, "Bring him on in, fellas."

"All right, Sergeant."

Tom noted that his father was now unconscious. "Put him there beside the wall." When he saw the colonel placed gently down, he said, "Thanks to you both. You fellas go on back and bring in the others. And I know there's plenty more that'll need to come here."

The ambulance driver looked doubtful. "Don't see that there's any room for 'em. Looks pretty bad, don't it, Sergeant?"

"Sure does."

Tom sat on the floor beside his father. From time to time he would go to the desk and urge the man in charge to get the colonel in to a surgeon. Each time he would be told that the operating room had a line waiting.

Finally Tom grew desperate. He left the waiting area and walked down the hall, his mind reeling, not knowing what to do. He saw a surgeon moving from one room to another, and he took a deep breath. "Sir," he said, "may I speak with you?"

The surgeon was a tall man with weary eyes. He appeared not to have slept in twenty-four hours. He had blood on his apron and looked tired enough to fall over.

"I've got my father outside—Colonel Nelson Majors. He's got a bullet in his side. Sir, if it doesn't come out, he'll die."

The surgeon stared at him hard. "Your father, you say?"

"That's right, I'm Tom Majors."

"You his aide?"

"Well, that's all I can do now." Tom tapped his wooden leg. "I lost this leg at Gettysburg, so I just have to do what I can for the cause."

The surgeon hesitated. "I guess I can help you some. Have them bring him into this room right here. I'll take the bullet out."

An hour later, when the bullet had been removed and Tom was sitting beside his father, the surgeon said wearily, "The wound wasn't too bad. But the trouble with these wounds is that sometimes the bullets carry parts of clothing or metal inside the body—or we don't get all the bullet. Then it festers, and blood poisoning sets in. That's what you have to watch out for."

"Thank you, sir. I'll take care of him."

"You'll have to, son. It looks like all the nurses and doctors around here have got all they can do."

The next twelve hours were a nightmare. Tom did the best he could for his father, but by the end of that time he saw that the colonel's fever was rising. When daylight came, he went again to try to get help. He found the surgeon in charge to be a surly, fat man named Washington.

"Dr. Washington," Tom said, "my father's got a high fever."

"I can't be bothered with that! I've got bullets to take out of men . . . legs to cut off . . ."

"But he's going to die!"

"A lot of these men are going to die," Dr. Washington said. "You'll just have to do the best you can." He hustled off, leaving Tom staring after him, anger in his eyes.

He waited in line at the well for an hour. Then he returned to his father and mopped the colonel's face with water. The colonel's fever had risen further, and he was mumbling under his breath.

Tom was frantic. "I've got to do something! He'll die if he doesn't get better care than this." *God*, he prayed silently, *show me what to do.*

He sat studying his father's face, and then suddenly a thought came to him. His lips tightened, and he said, "I'm going to try it, Pa!"

He stood up and grabbed a passing attendant by the arm. Tom was a strong man, and the attendant was small. He winced as Tom held onto him, increasing his grip. "That's my father, and he's Colonel Nelson Majors. You take care of him until I get back, or I'll turn you wrong side out. You hear me?"

The attendant, a mousy-looking man, saw the look in the tall soldier's eye. "Why, sure, Sergeant, I'll be glad to," he said. He immediately sat down beside the colonel. "I'll wait right here."

"Be sure you do!" Tom growled. He wheeled and left the room, making plans and assured that the timid attendant would stay right beside his father.

11
"Go Get Eileen"

The banging of fists on the door brought Leah out of a sound sleep with a start. She sat straight up and stared around wildly, convinced for the moment that she was having a nightmare. The room was barely illuminated by a sliver of moon that poured faint, silvery gleams over the bedclothes and the walls. Sitting there with jumbled thoughts racing through her mind—confused and a little afraid—Leah rubbed her eyes.

The insistent banging came again.

Slipping out of bed, she grabbed a robe and put it about her shoulders. Outside her bedroom door she met Eileen, who had come from her own room down the hall.

"What is it?" Leah asked.

"It must be news about the battle," Eileen whispered.

Leah stared at the front door with dread. She knew that she and Eileen were thinking the same thing—death had come for one of the Majorses.

Quickly Eileen went to the door and put her hand on the key. "Who is it?"

"It's me—Tom Majors."

Eileen turned the key and flung the door back. She took one glance at Tom's face and said, "What is it, Tom?"

"It's Pa." The young man's face was twisted with

grief. "He got shot, and I brought him back to Chimborazo."

"Oh, Tom," Leah whispered. She put a hand on his arm. "Is it bad?"

"Bad enough, I reckon," Tom said grimly. "They got the bullet out, but he's got infection, I'm afraid."

"What did the doctor say?"

Anger raced across Tom's countenance. "They don't say much of anything! To tell the truth, most of 'em are so busy they don't know what they're doing, and the aides run around like crazy men."

"What about the nurses?"

"There's not enough of 'em, and Pa's awful sick."

"Come in, Tom," Eileen said, stepping back. "Come into the sitting room and tell us about it." She led the way, lit a lamp, and then sat in a chair, clutching her robe around her. "Tell us everything. How did it happen?"

Tom began sketching the battle. He interrupted his story once to say, "Jeff is all right. Jeff done good."

"Is he still there, or did he come back with you?"

"We had to leave him there. We need every man we can get," he said gravely. "If it hadn't been for this leg, I'd have sent *him* with Pa, but he's a better man than I am right now."

"What about Nelson's wound?"

"It took him in the side, and the doctor said he was afraid somethin' got carried in with the musket ball. Maybe some wool cloth from the uniform, or maybe a piece of the bullet broke off. In any case, it's all turned inflamed, and I don't know what to do. And the doctors, they're about crazy trying to do their job. But the one that's in charge of Pa's ward, he's the worst of all."

Eileen sat listening, her hands clenched tightly

112

together. Her face grew tense as she listened to Tom's doleful report of how poorly his father was doing. When he finished, she said, "I'll go back with you, Tom."

An expression of relief swept across his face. "That's why I came," he confessed. He ran his hands through his black hair. "I was prayin', trying to think of what to do, and it came to me: *Go get Eileen.* I don't know if it was from the Lord or not, but I don't see how it could've come from anywhere else."

"Of course, I'll go. Leah, you'll have to stay here and take care of Esther . . ."

"Yes, but I wish I could go too."

"Your job is here," Eileen said. "We'll get back as quick as we can." She jumped up and left the room without another word.

Tom stared after her with admiration. "She is some punkins, Eileen Fremont."

"Your pa thinks so," Leah said quietly.

They waited while Eileen dressed, and as soon as she came back, bearing a small suitcase, all three went to the door.

"I borrowed a wagon for us to go in, Eileen," Tom said. "I'll bring you back after you've seen Pa."

"We'll see about that," Eileen said firmly. Then she kissed Leah. "I wish I could say good-bye to Esther."

"I'll give her a kiss for you," Leah said. "And I'll be praying for your father, Tom."

"He needs all the prayer he can get." Tom opened the door.

Leah watched Tom help Eileen into the wagon. As it rumbled away, she leaned against the door

113

frame. Her thoughts were on the colonel, but she also thought about Jeff, who had been left back at the battle. A sick feeling came over her as she realized that he could be killed at any time. She remembered how badly she had behaved toward him, and she whispered, "Just let him be all right, Lord, and I'll never act like that again."

Eileen marched into the room where Nelson Majors lay on a cot. She had to squeeze past the other beds, and two men were lying on the floor. A terrible odor was in the air. None of the men seemed to have been cared for. She said quietly, "This is awful, Tom."

"It is for a fact, but maybe we can get him cleaned up at least."

"We can certainly do that. Let's get some water." She knelt beside the bed and pulled back the cover.

The colonel's eyes opened, and he stared at her blankly.

"Nelson, are you awake?"

"Guess so."

His voice was so faint that Eileen had to lean forward. "You're going to be all right." She brushed his black hair back from his brow. He was burning up with fever, she realized, and she whispered, "I'm here to take care of you now."

"Eileen . . ."

"Yes, it's Eileen. You rest now. You'll be all right, Nelson."

For the next hour, Eileen gave commands. She ordered Tom around. She commandeered two aides and threatened them with violence if they did not help her get the entire room cleaned up. The wounded men were made more comfortable, and she went from one to another, changing bandages. Finally she came back to Nelson after sending Tom out for two more buckets of fresh water.

"We've got to get that fever down, Tom," she said when he returned. "Here, help me."

"All right, Eileen. I don't know anything about it, so you're the doctor."

Together they kept damp cloths on the colonel's body, and slowly the fever went down.

"I think he's better," Tom said with relief.

Eileen wiped her brow with the apron she had put on. It was so hot she could barely breathe, and there was only one small window.

At that moment, a surgeon passed by the door, and Tom said, "There's Dr. Washington, if you want to see him. I don't think he's gonna do much, though."

Eileen jumped to her feet and ran to the door. "Doctor!" she said clearly. When he turned, she said, "These men have got to have better care."

"And who are you?"

"My name is Eileen Fremont. I've come to take care of Colonel Majors."

"Who sent you here? What's your authority?"

"My authority is from God, who tells us to care for the sick. I think that's at least as strong as yours, Doctor!"

Dr. Washington began to yell. "Get out of this hospital! I'll have you know I'm in charge here . . ."

However, the doctor had apparently never met a woman exactly like Eileen Fremont. She stood listening to him, but even before he quit, she felt anger boiling up in her. She had had trouble with temper all her life in moments of crisis, but now the thought of helpless men being in the care of this incompetent braggart infuriated her.

"I wonder what President Davis would think if he knew that the wounded men under your charge were being left to wallow in their own filth. Perhaps I should just let him know about it!"

Washington's eyes blinked, but he said, "President Davis? You don't know President Davis!"

"Do I not? You'll find out how much I know him!" This was all a bluff on Eileen's part. The president of the Confederacy did not know she existed— but Dr. Washington could not be sure of that. "Perhaps I should go prove to you how firm our president can be. Maybe he'll find a place for you on the front lines, Doctor."

She got as far as the door to the waiting area when Washington's voice caught her. "Wait a minute," he said. "Wait just a minute, can't you? Don't push a man like that."

Eileen turned and waited. "Well, what are you going to do about these men?"

"We're doing the best we can, ma'am. As you can see, we've got too many sick men here to care for."

"I can see that already," Eileen conceded. She thought quickly and said, "I think it might be better if I took Colonel Majors to my home. He can be better cared for there than here."

Relief washed over the doctor's face. "If you've got a place for him, that might be best. Many of the men have already been taken in by the good people of Richmond. Let me get you an ambulance, and I'll have two men go to help you with him."

"We already have an army ambulance. But the help would be good, Doctor. And the men can bring the wagon back."

Washington issued orders quickly, and soon Nelson Majors was lying inside Tom's wagon.

Eileen turned to the doctor, feeling bad about the way she had bullied him. "I'm sorry I lost my temper, Dr. Washington," she said quietly. "It's just that I'm so concerned about these men. It's been hard on you, I'm sure, and you have an awful responsibility."

Washington swallowed and said, "It's kind of you to say so, ma'am. And I'll do my best to see that the men have as good care as we can offer. It'll help a lot, though, for you to care for the colonel by yourself. There's really nothing I can do here that you can't do there."

"Good-bye, Doctor, and God bless you."

Feeling somewhat better, Dr. Washington lingered at the door to watch the woman and her wagon leave the hospital. *That is some red-haired lady,* he thought. *I hope that colonel appreciates her.*

Leah stood outside and watched the army ambulance pull up in front of Uncle Silas's house. Without waiting for help, Eileen leaped to the ground. Then she supervised the men carrying the colonel to the door.

"I got a bed all made up in case you'd bring him," Leah said. "I gave him the front room, Eileen—it's got more breeze there."

"That's good, Leah," Eileen said. "Come this way." She marched into the front bedroom. "Put him in the bed there!" she commanded.

"Yes, ma'am!" The two men handled the limp form of Nelson Majors carefully and laid him on the bed.

Eileen said, "Thank you very much. I appreciate your help."

"No trouble, ma'am."

As soon as the men were gone, Eileen and Leah went to either side of the bed.

The colonel's eyes had been closed, but he opened them. He looked up and blinked, then whispered hoarsely. "Is that you, Eileen?"

"It's me, Nelson. You're home now." She brushed his hair back and felt his forehead. "Your fever's coming up again. We'll have to keep it down."

"I'm a lot of trouble."

Eileen Fremont kept her hand on his forehead. "How could you be that, Nelson?" she whispered.

Leah watched as the two looked at each other. Colonel Majors was very sick, but she noticed that when he reached out his hand and Eileen took it, that seemed to give him relief.

Leah said, "I'll go get some water, and we can start the cool baths." As she left, she thought, *It's a good thing Eileen's here. I think God must've sent her for just this reason. I wish Jeff knew about it.*

12

The Battle of the Crater

Jeff raised his head slightly over the log that lay at the top of the trench where he crouched. He did it slowly because a good friend had done the same thing a week earlier and had the top of his head blown off. Both Confederate and Union troops had grown respectful of the sharpshooters.

The Yankees lay in trenches much like the one he was in, less than four hundred feet away, and everywhere Jeff looked there was a vast maze of tunnels, trenches, and fortifications.

Slipping back down into the trench, he joined the rest of the squad, who looked as tired, grimy, and disgusted as he was. "Well, I didn't see anything," he said.

"I reckon you won't see much." Sergeant Mapes spat tobacco juice down at his feet. "Even the Yankees got more sense than to attack against this kind of defense."

"I don't know what makes you think that!" Curly Henson remarked. He had a pack of homemade playing cards and was playing poker with Jed Hawkins. "They always done it afore!"

Mapes shook his head. "Yeah, but I saw in the newspaper that the Yankees done lost seventy thousand men since they hit us at the Wilderness."

Jeff looked up with astonishment. "Seventy thousand men *dead?*"

"Not all of them dead," Mapes said. "Some of 'em wounded, some just missin'." He spat an amber stream of juice again. "We can't go at them, and they can't go at us."

"I don't like this kind of life," Jed Hawkins said. He looked at his hand of cards, threw it down, and picked up his guitar. Somehow Jed always managed to have his guitar with him, even in the midst of battle. He strummed for a while, then began to sing. His clear, tenor voice rose over the trenches so that likely even the Federals, lying nearby, could hear him:

"Wounded and sorrowful, far from my home,
Sick among strangers, uncared for, unknown;
Even the birds that used sweetly to sing
Are silent and swiftly have taken the wing.
No one but Mother can cheer me today,
No one for me could so fervently pray;
None to console me, no kind friend is near;
Mother would comfort me if she were here!"

Jeff gave Jed a disgusted look. "I swear, that's a mournful tune! Don't you know any happy songs about soldiers?"

"Ain't any." Jed grinned at him crookedly. He sang another verse. Then he laid the guitar down and began to walk along the trench, careful to bend over. He was met by another man who was carrying a bucket. Hawkins said, "Looks like it's dinnertime. What's in this, Cookie?"

"Don't ask," the cook said grimly. "You'll be better off not knowin'." He surrendered the bucket, and Jed returned with it. "Get your mess gear out. Time for our usual seven-course dinner."

Jeff picked up his tin plate and held it out while Hawkins spooned some sort of stew onto it. As soon as he got it, he ducked back and sat leaning against the earth trench. He tasted the stew, and Charlie Bowers, sitting across from him, said, "What does it taste like, Jeff?"

"It tastes like fox to me."

Charlie stared at him. "What does a fox taste like?"

"About like an owl." Jeff grinned. "I don't know what it is, Charlie. Probably mule. Just eat it, and don't ask any questions."

The men ate hungrily, for at least it was food, and men had to eat. The daily ration of meat amounted usually to three or four ounces, about a mouthful per man. Food boxes from home had stopped now that the Confederates had been cut off by the siege line. An Irish member of Parliament, who had come to visit the Confederates, had dinner with General Lee; he reported to those back home, "He had two biscuits, and he gave me one."

In the trenches, constant skirmishing and sharp-shooting took their deadly toll. Continual shelling back and forth raked the nerves of all the men. The heat was terrible, and dust, alternating with mud, made the situation worse. The mud and the filth brought disease, and some of their friends had died. More friends had died of disease than of musket balls. Jeff had seen strong men sink into apathy and brood for hours.

He finished his stew, wiped his plate with a handkerchief that was none too clean, and said, "I'm goin' down the line to see what's happenin'."

Sergeant Mapes gave him a questioning look.

"The same thing that's happening here—nothing!" he said.

But Jeff was restless and got up, careful to keep his body in a crouch so that none of it showed over the top of the logs that lined the trenches. He had gone no more than five steps when suddenly he was knocked completely off his feet. A tremendous roar half deafened him, and he thought with shock, *A shell's gone off in the trench!*

He lay facedown in the dirt for a moment, wondering if he had been hit, then he struggled to his feet. But no sooner had he done so than dirt, dust, and wooden objects began to rain down upon him. Something struck him on the shoulder but caused no damage.

"What's goin' on?" he cried.

"Don't know!" Sergeant Mapes said. He, too, was dodging the raining dirt. "A bomb must've gone off. Ain't no shell can do that! It looks like it hit down the line."

By now all the troops were scrambling to their feet and staring with amazement to their left.

"Look at that, will you!" Curly Henson said with awe.

Jeff looked, along with the others, and saw a huge cloud of dust and debris rising in a column. Some of it was already beginning to fall on the part of the trench where he was. "What kind of a shell would do *that?*" he asked.

No one answered, for no one knew of a shell that big. What they did not know was that the gigantic explosion was a result of work by a Colonel Pleasance. This Federal colonel was a mining engineer, and many of his men who came from Pennsylvania had been miners. Pleasance had watched the futile efforts of his officers to break the Confederate resistance. When all else failed, he came up with the idea of tunneling underground and planting a huge charge of powder under the Confederate line.

With tremendous effort, a tunnel more than five hundred feet long was dug. When it was completed, eight thousand pounds of black powder were placed at the end of it. A hundred-foot fuse was attached to the powder and lighted. It burned out. Two men went back in to relight it. Finally, the powder had gone off.

The hole blasted by the huge charge was enormous. Federal troops, black soldiers under General Ferrero, started to enter. But the Confederates, after the first shock, began to rush toward the huge, gaping crater.

Officers shouted commands. "Put your men on the edge of that crater!" And that was what the following battle would be called: the Battle of the Crater.

"Come on!" Sergeant Mapes yelled.

Rubble was still swirling in the air, and dust was thick, but Jeff could see the enemy flooding into the break. He grabbed up an extra musket. Every man counted. With a hole in the Confederate line, the Yankees could rush in and Richmond would be taken.

"It's a good thing for us they don't have ladders," he said. "But look! Look! They can't get up out of the hole!"

Anyone looking down could see that this was true. The Federals had poured into the huge crater, but they could not get out because the sides were so steep.

Muskets began to go off, and Union soldiers began to fall. Jeff felt bad about it. "Like shooting fish in a barrel," he muttered. But more and more Union soldiers kept coming, and the line had to be held.

The battle grew hot, and the bottom of the crater was a terrible thing to see. The sun blazed down on it with fierce heat. Men were dying everywhere. And at last the Federals drew back.

The Confederate victory was almost completely won when Jeff suddenly felt a blow on his left arm. He supposed for a moment that Ocie had struck him, and he turned to say something. But then he fell to the ground and thought with astonishment, *Why, I've been shot!*

Jeff felt no pain, but his whole arm was numb. He looked down, saw bright red blood gushing, and desperately put his hand over the wound. But the bleeding did not stop.

"Jeff, you've been hit!"

Ocie threw down his musket and leaped to kneel beside him. "You're gonna bleed to death!"

Jeff tried to speak, but the shock was too great. He watched as Ocie whipped off his belt and quickly wrapped it around his arm. Then he saw that the blood had stopped running so freely.

"Hey, you fellas! Jeff's been hit! Help me get him back!" Ocie cried.

Jed Hawkins took one look and said, "Can you walk, Jeff?"

"I—I reckon I can," he managed to say.

Jeff was able to get to his feet. Ocie kept the belt tied around his arm, and soon they were back behind the lines, where a tall, skinny doctor said, "Sit down there. I'll have to patch you up."

Jeff then knew pain, for feeling returned to his arm, but he kept his lips clamped tightly together.

When the doctor finished treating him, he said, "You'll be OK. Didn't break the bone, or I'd have had to take that arm off." Before leaving, he looked down again and grinned. "Whoever put that belt around your arm saved your life, soldier."

Jeff looked at Ocie. He was faint from the loss of blood, and Ocie's face seemed to be wavering. "I guess you saved my life, Ocie."

"Well, you saved mine back in the Wilderness, and turnabout's fair play." Ocie was looking much relieved. "I thought you was a goner, Jeff. How do you feel?"

"OK." He lay quietly, his head swimming, and he felt slightly nauseated. Ocie got him a drink of water, and when he had sipped it he said, "You know, I think maybe God had all this figured out."

"What do you mean, Jeff?"

"I mean He knew I was gonna have to have some help. So that's why I went to get you out of that fire back in the Wilderness."

Ocie thought about that. "Well, it's nice to have somebody to take care of us. Like the Scripture says, two are better than one."

Jeff felt himself slipping into unconsciousness, and he whispered, "Yes, two are better than one, Ocie . . ."

Jeff cautiously got down out of the ambulance and waved at the driver. "Thanks for the ride," he said.

The driver stepped down and nodded at him. "You got off easy. Some of those we got in here are a lot worse off."

"I know it," Jeff said soberly.

He was still weak and had developed a slight fever, but finally the doctors had told him, "Go home. Go back to Richmond and get healed up. Then you can come back and fight some more. Get shot in the other arm, maybe."

Jeff had said, "I don't think I want to try that." But he'd come home to Richmond, and now he was looking for his father. He had not heard about the colonel and feared he might not have survived.

He walked into the long, low building that the driver had told him was headquarters for Chimborazo. A woman sat behind a desk.

"I'm looking for Colonel Nelson Majors."

"Nelson Majors?" The woman picked up a notebook and leafed through it. "He's in Ward G. That's out the door to your left."

"Thanks, ma'am."

Jeff left the office, turned left, and made his way down the hallway.

When he got to Ward G, he stepped inside. The ward was lined on both sides with cots, all of them occupied, except for those where the men were able to walk about. A stubby man in rather dirty clothes was mopping the floor.

Jeff said to him, "I'm looking for Colonel Majors."

The man immediately stopped mopping and leaned on the mop handle. It was as if he had been looking for an excuse to quit work. "Colonel Majors? Why, he ain't here!"

Apprehension shot through Jeff. *He's dead!* he thought. He swallowed hard and said, "Where is he?"

"Why, they come and took him!"

"*Who* took him?"

"A redheaded woman! I was standing right here when she come in and bucked up against Dr. Washington." He wheezed and laughed silently. "She told him off, she did. Like nobody else. Said he wasn't fit to doctor hogs."

Relief flooded through Jeff. "Was the woman's name Mrs. Fremont?"

"I think that's what she said. She had another soldier with her. A sergeant."

"That was my brother." Jeff nodded. "Where did they take him?"

"Said they was takin' him back home. I reckon you might know where that is?"

"Yes, I know. Thanks a lot." Jeff left the ward, having to walk slowly. Besides feeling weak, he had had little to eat. "Don't know if I can get all the way out to Uncle Silas's house on foot," he said.

He started walking, however, and within five minutes a wagon pulled up beside him, a man and a woman on the seat.

"Hello, soldier!"

Jeff looked up. "Howdy! Sure could use a ride."

"You been fightin', have you?"

"Yes, got shot at the Crater."

"Where you goin'?" the woman asked, sympathy in her eyes.

"I'm goin' to Silas Carter's house in the country."

The woman's eyes opened with surprise. "Silas Carter? Why, he's a neighbor of ours."

"Sure is," the man said. He was heavyset and almost spilled out of his clothes. "Get in here! Move over, Eulah. Make room for that soldier."

With some difficulty Jeff climbed up and sat in the back of the wagon.

The man spoke to the horses, and they moved forward again.

"You know Silas ain't home, don't you?"

"Yes, I know that, but I think my father's there."

"I did hear somethin' about that," the woman said. "I ain't met your father, of course."

Grateful for the ride, Jeff swayed with the wagon. He was thinking about what the orderly had said—that Eileen Fremont had just about saved his father's life.

He answered the questions the couple put to him, but his mind was ranging ahead. *If she saved Pa's life, I'll sure be grateful to her as long as I live.*

13
Jeff Changes His Mind

Getting down from the wagon, Jeff looked up at the friendly couple and smiled. "Sure do thank you for the ride. I don't think I could've made it without you!"

"Why, it's little enough to do for one of our heroes," the woman said, smiling back.

Jeff shook his head. "Don't reckon I'm much of a hero."

"You are to us," the man said. "Anybody that keeps the Yankees out of Richmond is a hero. Do you think we can keep 'em out much longer?"

Jeff had no answer and said merely, "I hope so. Well, thanks again."

"You're welcome, soldier. May God be with you."

As the wagon moved on, he started toward the house. He had not had anything to eat since the previous day, and his arm was hurting fiercely. The doctor had bound it up and put it in a sling, but there had been no pain medication to give him.

"Jeff!"

Leah sailed out the door. Her eyes were wide, and her hair floated behind her as she ran to him.

"Jeff, are you all right?"

"Sure," he said. He managed a grin. "I got shot, but it wasn't too bad."

Leah's eye flew to the sling. "Come on in the house and sit down."

"Reckon I'd be ready for that," Jeff said wearily. His head began to swim, and he staggered slightly.

She reached for him, saying quickly, "Lean on me, Jeff."

"Guess I'll have to." Jeff put his right arm around her shoulders, and she helped him across the yard. As they went up the steps, he grew even more dizzy and said, "I don't . . . know if I can make it, Leah."

"Just a few more steps," she urged. She was practically shoving him up the last step when the door opened and Eileen came out. She took one look and said, "Here, let's get him inside. Jeff, you're white as a sheet."

"Don't feel too good," he muttered.

The two women maneuvered him through the door and into the sitting room, where they put him into an upholstered horsehide chair.

Jeff laid his head back against the cushion and whispered, "Thanks. Good thing it wasn't farther."

"Have you had anything to eat?" Leah asked.

"Yesterday."

"Leah, you stay with him. He needs some water, and I'll fix him some broth. I'll go out and kill a chicken."

Jeff heard, but his eyes were closed, and he felt as though he was going to lose consciousness. He felt Leah's hand on his head.

"Have you had a fever?"

"Thought I was over it," he mumbled. "I guess not."

"You'll be all right now that you're home. We'll take care of you, Eileen and me."

"How's Pa?" Jeff asked. When no answer came, he opened his eyes and saw the worried look on

Leah's face. Instantly he straightened up, the movement sending pain through his wounded arm. "He's not dead, is he?"

"Oh, no! He's not dead, Jeff. He's just not as well as we'd like."

"What about the bullet?"

"Well, the doctor took that out. But there's been some kind of infection, and he can't seem to shake off the fever. Can't eat much."

"I want to see him."

He struggled to get up, but Leah firmly pushed his head back. "You lie right there! You're a patient too, now, so you'll have to mind what I say."

Jeff studied her through slitted eyes. A smile pulled at his lips, and he whispered, "I guess you'll like that. You always did want to boss me around."

Leah seemed truly worried about him. He supposed he had lost weight and that his face was paler than she had ever seen it. She pulled his cap off and smoothed his hair back. "You're awfully dirty," she said.

"Not many places to take a bath out on the lines," he defended himself. "Tell me more about Pa."

"I'll tell you just a little, and then we're going to get you fed and cleaned up."

Jeff, in all truthfulness, did not feel like arguing. He sat there, quietly listening to Leah tell how Eileen and Tom had practically kidnapped his father from the hospital.

"You would have been proud of her, Jeff, from what Tom said."

"The orderly remembered her too. Said she was like a redheaded drill sergeant. Really told the doctor off."

"She's a wonderful nurse. I would have been scared to death if she hadn't been here. She's taking such good care of your father—hardly ever leaves his side."

Shortly after that, Jeff dropped off to sleep. When he awoke, there was a wonderful smell of food, and he opened his eyes.

Eileen stood before him with a large, steaming bowl. "Now, can you feed yourself?"

"Why, of course I can, Mrs. Fremont!" He proved it by sitting up and eating the entire bowl of chicken broth with the large spoon she gave him.

Both women watched him, giving him pieces of cornbread from time to time.

When he was finished, he said, "That was the best thing I've had to eat in a month—since we left here! Can I see Pa now?"

"No, we're going to get you cleaned up."

"I can clean myself up!" Jeff protested. He had no choice over the matter, however, for soon he was stripped to the waist and being bathed gently but firmly by both women. And then the dressing on his arm was changed.

"You can have one of Tom's shirts. It'll be a little bit large," Leah said. She helped Jeff into it and put the sling back on. "Now, I think he can see his father. Don't you think so, Eileen?"

"Come along. We'll see if he's awake."

Jeff got up carefully, and when Leah took his arm, he protested again. "You don't have to help me!"

"Hush, Jeff! I don't want to hear anything else out of you. I've been so worried about you, and now I've got a chance to take care of you, so you might as well be quiet!"

Actually Jeff liked the attention, but he muttered, "Makes a fella feel like a baby!"

The trio moved down the hall and through a doorway, and Jeff saw his father lying flat on the bed. His face was pale, but his eyes were open. "Jeff!" he whispered. "Are you all right?"

Jeff, with Leah's help, moved over beside the bed where a chair was shoved under him. "Sure, I'm all right, Pa. Got a little nick. Nothin' serious. How are you?"

Nelson Majors's cheeks were sunken, and so were his eyes. His skin was pale and sallow. "Well, to tell the truth, I have felt better," he murmured. Then he looked over at Eileen and tried to grin. "But if it wasn't for this lady here and Leah, I'd be feeling a lot worse—or not feeling at all."

"You'll be all right, Nelson," Eileen said. "Now you have a good talk with Jeff while I go fix you something special to eat."

The women left, and Jeff sat beside his father. The colonel seemed tired and would drop off to sleep for short periods of time, sometimes only for a few seconds.

"Can't seem to stay awake." He half laughed. Then he said, "Tell me about the battle. How'd you get shot?"

Jeff told him about the Battle of the Crater, describing it as well as he could.

By the time he had finished, Leah and Eileen were back. They had brought a soup of some sort of meat that had been boiled until it fell apart.

"Let me help you up, Nelson." With surprising strength for one so small, Eileen set the big man upright. She fluffed the pillow behind him and said,

"Now, you're going to eat every bite of this if I have to shove it down your throat!"

Nelson winked at his son. "That's the way they treat a fellow, Jeff. I got no rights at all around here."

"I think you better mind her. From what I heard, she's a bad woman to cross."

Eileen had a forkful of meat poised before the colonel's lips, but at Jeff's words she turned toward him.

Jeff smiled. It was the first time that he had ever smiled at her, as far as he could remember.

She smiled back. "I guess I behaved pretty badly at the hospital."

"Tom thought she was gonna cut that doctor's gizzard out," Jeff said. "He said he had to hold her back to keep her from pullin' him baldheaded."

"He didn't say any such thing!" Eileen protested, blushing.

Now everybody was laughing at Mrs. Fremont, and she grew flustered. "A person does what they have to do!" she said firmly. Then she shoved the meat into Nelson's mouth, saying, "Now, you chew on that and chew it up good."

Late that afternoon, Jeff, sitting in a rocking chair on the front porch, saw a horseman coming. Soon he recognized the rider and hollered, "Tom! It's me!"

Tom Majors swung off the horse, tied it to the hitching post, and came onto the porch. His limp was noticeable, but it was not bad. He grinned and clapped Jeff on his good shoulder. "Well, you managed to get yourself a free pass to Richmond, I see."

"Pretty sorry way to get a pass, I'd say," Jeff said. "What's up with you, Tom?"

"I'll be a messenger from now on. Don't need two legs to ride a horse." He took the chair beside Jeff, and once again Jeff told the story of the Battle of the Crater.

When he had finished, Tom said, "I'm glad you're all right, Jeff. How's the arm?"

"Oh, it's a little stiff and hurts some, but the doctor said it'd be all right."

"You've got a good nurse. I don't know a better one than Eileen, and Leah's a good helper."

When Tom went inside to wash up, Leah came out onto the porch and sat on the steps close to Jeff. She looked up at him. "How does your arm feel?"

"Feels great!" Jeff said cheerfully. "As long as I don't bang it or do anything with it."

"I hope the war's over by the time it gets well."

"I doubt that it will be."

Leah looked in the direction of Petersburg, where the boys had been, as if she could hear the guns. "It's pretty bad in the trenches, isn't it?"

Jeff did not answer for a moment, but then he nodded. "Pretty bad."

"Do you think there's any way we can win?"

Jeff looked down at his feet. "I don't think so," he said at last. "But we got to go on."

"I wish the South would quit. I'd hate to see another man lost from the North *or* the South."

Suddenly Jeff knew that was what he wished too, but he could not say so. That would appear disloyal. "Well," he said, "it'll be over one way or another pretty soon."

Talking quietly, they watched the sun slowly descend.

Jeff said, "Sounds like if it hadn't been for Mrs. Fremont, Pa wouldn't have made it."

"That's right," Leah agreed. "I think she saved his life. So many men have died in that hospital just from being overcrowded and not getting enough care."

"Seems like he's getting good enough care here."

"Have you changed your mind about Eileen?" Leah asked. She studied his face.

Jeff lowered his head for a moment, then lifted his eyes to meet hers. "A fella can't be mad at somebody who takes good care of his pa, maybe saves his life."

Leah smiled. "I'm glad you feel that way. She's really a fine woman."

While Jeff and Leah talked on the front porch, Eileen was giving her patient a haircut. She had come in with a pair of scissors and without preamble said, "You're getting your hair cut."

Nelson struggled to a sitting position, and she helped him to a chair. When he was seated comfortably, she put a towel around his neck. Then, taking comb and scissors, she said, "Now, you be still, or I might cut your ears off!"

"Don't see why I need a haircut. I'm not going to see anybody," he protested.

"You're going to see me, and I'm going to see you. I don't want you looking like some kind of wild hillbilly!"

The colonel sat quietly as Eileen began to work on his hair. Surprisingly, his fever was down, and he felt better than he had in some time. As she moved around in front of him, her eyes on his hair, he was able to study her face. She had smooth skin and an attractiveness about her features that he had rarely seen. Without planning to, he said, "You're a very attractive woman, Eileen."

"What?" She stopped abruptly. Her face was only a few inches from his, and she flushed. "Well, thank you," she said.

He thought for a moment that he'd gone too far. "I didn't mean to offend you."

Eileen smiled, reached out and cut a lock, then said, "I don't suppose you can offend a woman by telling her she looks nice." She continued to work, and her hands were light as she brushed the clipped hair away. "I'm going to trim your mustache too. It's getting too woolly. Be still!"

She worked swiftly and carefully. "Now, a shave. I'm not sure about that. I'm not really a barber."

"I'd appreciate it. Never did like to let a shave go. It makes my face itch."

For the next ten minutes he sat quietly as she lathered his face and soaked it, then began to shave him with a straight razor.

"Don't move!" she warned. "One wound's enough!"

He could not help grinning. "More than enough, I'd say!" He sat still until she had finished and had wiped his face. She was leaning over him when all of a sudden he reached out, pulled her close, and kissed her soundly.

When he let her go, she stood up gasping. "Why, Nelson Majors!" she exclaimed. "What made you do such a thing?"

"I always kiss pretty nurses every chance I get. It's the only way I can repay them for what they've done."

"You certainly seem better! Well, you just behave yourself." She put the shaving gear away. Then she sat in the chair beside him, picked up a book, and began reading to him. But a thought seemed to come to her, and she laid down the book. "You know, if I'd been able to nurse my husband as I have you, Nelson, he might not have died."

"I truly wish he hadn't, Eileen."

She looked up quickly, as though to determine if he was serious. "I'm glad I was here to help you."

"I'm glad too." He lowered his head and said, "I thought I'd never find another woman as kind as my first wife, but I have."

He reached out a hand, and she took it. For a long time they just sat holding hands, saying nothing. Eileen may not have known what this meant, but she seemed content.

He wondered what would happen to the two of them.

Outside, Jeff stirred. "I guess she's done a lot for him, hasn't she, Leah?"

"I think she loves him, Jeff," Leah said quietly, "and love isn't ever selfish."

14
A Woman of Strength

Gen. Robert E. Lee was not a man to demand high honors for himself. As the siege of Petersburg went on, he refused to make his headquarters inside a house. Instead, he chose to have his tent pitched in a yard, refusing all the many offers made to him. It was from there that Lee wrote to his wife early in June, reminding her that their thirty-third anniversary was approaching and speaking wistfully of that happy day.

Inside Petersburg, men and women went about their daily business, although shells fell frequently. Sometimes they blew houses to bits and tore up the streets. Around the city, twenty-six miles of fortifications kept the Federals out, and work on them never stopped.

The Union Army also built fortifications, and the weary weeks passed slowly for both sides.

Bad news continued to come from outside Petersburg, for the Confederacy was losing ground daily. Word came that Farragut's fleet had entered Mobile Bay and closed that Southern seaport. Word also came that General Sherman's army had taken Atlanta and would soon be marching to the sea.

Inside Richmond, too, things continued to worsen. Prices skyrocketed. Confederate money was worth practically nothing. One inhabitant said, "I saw selling at auction today secondhand shirts at forty dollars each, and blankets at seventy-five dollars each. A bedstead such as I bought for ten dollars brought seven hundred dollars."

One issue that came up was the question of using slaves as soldiers. Lee himself was in favor of it. He said in a letter, "My own opinion is that we should employ them without delay. I believe with proper regulations they can be made efficient soldiers." He also felt that any slave who fought in the army should be given his freedom, which did not set well with many people.

Jeff found use for himself in Richmond. His arm was still in a sling, but he had grown healthy under the persistent care of Eileen Fremont and Leah. He found that he could work in the garden, which supplied most of the food for their small household.

One late afternoon he was out picking butter beans when he looked up to see Tom riding in. Tom had come and gone with regularity, having adapted himself well to serving in the cavalry.

Leah was in the garden with Jeff, wearing an old green-and-white dress and a bonnet to shade her face.

"I'm right proud of Tom, Leah," he said quietly as his brother rode up. "I think he's going to be all right."

Leah straightened up and watched Jeff's brother swing from the saddle almost as gracefully as he had once done with two good legs. "He looks fine, doesn't he?"

"Does he ever write to Sarah?"

"I don't know, of course," she said. "Remember we haven't gotten any mail, and we won't as long we're pinned inside Richmond."

Jeff felt foolish, for he well knew that there was

no such thing as mail coming into the Southern capital.

Tom caught a glimpse of the pair and walked toward them. "Hello," he said. "Getting something good for supper?"

"Sure are, Tom," Jeff replied. "You gonna be able to stay?"

"I don't think so this time, but if you've got a few beans to put in a sack, I could take some back to the squad."

"Sure," Jeff said. "We'll be glad to. I know how good fresh vegetables taste when you're stuck out there in those trenches."

"I'll pick 'em up before I leave," Tom said. "Now, I better get inside and see Pa."

Tom knocked on the screen door, and almost at once Eileen was there. As she opened the door, Esther came catapulting out and grabbed Tom around the knees.

"Tom, come and play."

Laughing, he scooped up the child. As she prattled on, he compared her face with those memories he had of his mother. Turning to Eileen, he said, "She sure looks like Ma."

"That's good." Eileen smiled. "You'll always have something to remember her by. And every time she looks in the mirror, she'll know what her mother looked like."

Tom's eyes warmed. "That's a nice thought, Eileen." He had learned to admire Eileen Fremont. "I don't know what we would have done without you. I really don't."

"I'm glad I could be here."

"How's Pa today?"

"He's sitting up in the parlor."

"He is? Well, let me at him."

Tom followed her down the hall and turned off into the roomy sitting room. The two big windows at one end threw light down upon the form of Nelson Majors seated in an upholstered chair and holding a book in his lap. "Hey, Tom. I saw you ride in."

"Pa, good to see you up again." Still holding Esther, Tom walked over and shook his father's hand. Then he sat across from him, and the two began to chat.

Esther, however, would have none of that. "Play, Tom!" she said. "Play horsey!"

"All right." Tom laughed and knelt down. She got on his back, and he went around the room, tossing her with bends of his body.

The colonel watched his son play with the golden-haired child, and when Tom came back, out of breath, Nelson said, "That leg does pretty well."

"Better than I thought it would. I've got to thank Ezra a lot more than I have—and Leah too." Tom returned to his chair. "I was pretty stubborn about it, Pa. I thought I was going to be a worthless cripple the rest of my life. Now I feel like I can do just about anything."

"And that's good, Tom," his father said. "A man wants to be able to do for his family."

At the mention of family, Tom's eyes shot to his father. They had not talked about Sarah, but Tom knew that his father was thinking of her. Instead of mentioning Sarah, however, Tom said quickly, "I wish I had a million dollars. I'd give it to Eileen for taking over the way she has."

A warmth came to Nelson's face. "So would I. I don't know how to thank her."

"She's a fine woman," Tom remarked, playing with Esther's curls as she pawed at the bright buttons on his vest.

"Yes, she is."

"Good-lookin' too, don't you think?"

"I suppose so."

Tom laughed out loud. "You suppose so! You mean to tell me you haven't noticed?"

A flush mounted the older man's cheeks, and he grinned. "Well, I guess you'd have to say I have, Tom. After all, I may have been sick, but I haven't been dead."

Tom knew that his father had been lonely since the death of his wife, and now he asked casually, "Do you ever think of her as a woman you might marry?"

Silence fell over the room and continued so long that Tom was conscious of a fly buzzing around his head. He brushed it away and waited.

At length his father said quietly, "If I ever did marry again, I think she'd be the woman I'd like to have, but I'm worried about Jeff."

"Jeff? What's wrong with Jeff?"

"I think he's . . . well . . . jealous."

"Oh, he'll get over that, Pa. I mean, after all, he's grown almost. It's not like he was a baby. I'll talk to him."

"No, don't do that," the colonel said quickly. "Let me do it."

"All right, Pa."

That evening after supper, when Tom had gone back to camp and the colonel had moved back to his bed, Eileen was busy picking up a few things around the room.

143

Taking a deep breath, the colonel said, "Eileen, come over and sit down, will you?"

She shot him a quick glance and frowned at the look she saw on his face. "Why, what is it, Nelson?" She sat on the bedside chair. "Is something wrong?"

Nelson Majors was not the best man in the world with words. He knew what he wanted to say but somehow had become unable to put them in the right order. His eyes fell on the black Bible that lay on the table beside the bed, and he said, "Let me have that Bible, will you, Eileen? I want to read you something."

Opening the Book, he let his eyes run along the lines and began to read. His voice was low and pleasant as he read, "'Who can find a virtuous woman? for her price is far above rubies. The heart of her husband doth safely trust in her . . .'"

Eileen sat straight in her chair, her eyes fixed on his face. She listened as he read from the latter part of Proverbs 31: "'She looketh well to the ways of her household, and eateth not the bread of idleness. Her children arise up, and call her blessed; her husband also, and he praiseth her.'"

Nelson looked up at her suddenly and reached out and took her hand. "I'm not your husband— yet—but I'm afraid I'll have to take the words of Scripture."

"Why, whatever do you mean, Nelson?" Her breath seemed to come rather shortly.

His hand held hers tightly. "I'm afraid I'm going to have to praise you, Eileen Fremont. I've never seen a woman like you. If it hadn't been for you, I think I'd be dead by now." He looked down again and read another verse: "'Many daughters have done virtuously, but thou excellest them all. Favour

144

is deceitful, and beauty is vain: but a woman that feareth the Lord, she shall be praised.'"

After reading the last verse, he put his free hand on her cheek. "I will praise you, Eileen, for you have excelled above all women."

Eileen did not move for a moment. Then she leaned forward, and his lips met hers. Finally she drew back and said, "That was a lovely thing to say."

"I said no more than the truth. And I suppose you know what I want to say next, don't you?"

"What is it?"

"Would you marry me, Eileen, and be a wife to me and a mother to my children?"

Eileen lowered her eyes, her hand still in his as she said, "You know Jeff might be opposed. He doesn't like me very much."

"I'm not asking you to marry Jeff. He's almost a man now. He'll just have to get used to it. But I think he likes you more than you think. Things have been so shaken up in his life, he's just afraid of changes. I'll ask you again. Will you marry me, Eileen?"

The colonel knew that Eileen Fremont had not come to Richmond to get married. She had doubted seriously whether she would ever marry again.

But now, with her hand in his, the answer came quickly. "Yes," she said firmly, "I will marry you." She leaned over and kissed him again.

Neither the colonel nor Eileen was aware that Jeff had come to the door. He had heard nothing of what went on before. The sight of his father kissing Eileen disturbed him greatly. Quickly he tiptoed away, not wanting to make a scene. When he reached the kitchen, he started out the door, but Leah, washing potatoes at the sink, looked up and saw his face. "What's wrong, Jeff?"

"Nothing!" Jeff stomped outside and let the door slam. He plunged across the yard and had reached the well before Leah caught up with him.

Catching his arm, she turned him around. "Don't tell me there's nothing wrong!" she said sharply. "Your face is like a book, Jeff, and I can read it! Something's terribly wrong!"

Jeff looked at her in despair. "It's Pa," he said. "He was kissing her again."

"Well, what's wrong with *that?*"

"What's *wrong* with it?" Jeff exclaimed. Then he could not find an answer to his own question. He stood there struggling and could not say a word.

"Jeff, your father would have died if Eileen hadn't saved him—if she hadn't gotten him out of that hospital. And since then she's stayed up with him night after night, keeping his fever down. All you have to do is look at his face as he watches her to see that he loves her, and she loves him too."

Jeff was still upset. He said mulishly, "She shouldn't have been kissing him!"

"Jeff, don't talk to me any more about being a soldier. You're just a spoiled little boy! Afraid somebody will take his toys away from him! You're so selfish you don't even want your father to have the comfort that a man gets from a wife. Go along and play, little boy," she said scornfully. She walked away.

The screen door slammed, and he muttered, "Well, you don't have to get so sore about it!" He kicked at a stone, then stalked out into the twilight angry and upset—knowing somehow that he was in the wrong.

146

15
Birthday Party

Jeff plunged away off into the darkness and eventually found himself almost lost in the woods. He had planned to stay overnight at Silas's, not needing to go back to camp, but he felt so bad about the way he had behaved that he could not face either Leah or Eileen. Without going into the house to say good-bye to either of them, he returned to camp, where he stayed for the next two days.

Tom saw that he was in some sort of depression and tried to talk to him. "What's the matter with you, Jeff? You been going around with a face as long as a mule's. Are you sick?"

"No, I'm not sick!"

Tom stared at his younger brother. He knew him well enough to know that something was wrong. "Tomorrow is your birthday. Have you forgotten that?"

Strangely enough, Jeff *had* forgotten. "I guess I did," he said. "Well, what about it? It's just like every other day."

"No, it's not. You're going out to the house and have a birthday party. Leah and Eileen and Pa all asked me about it yesterday."

Jeff stared at his brother and then nodded. "OK, so I'll go."

"Well, that's mighty big of you. Doing them the favor of lettin' them bake you a cake and all that," Tom said, snorting. "You're acting like a baby, Jeff.

I'd like to know what's eatin' at you." He hesitated, appeared almost to say something, but then changed his mind. "I'll be off duty about three. We'll go out to the house together."

"All right, Tom."

The time ran by slowly for Jeff that morning. He thought a great deal about his father, remembering how devoted Pa had been to his mother. And then he thought a great deal about his mother, saddened by the memory as he always was.

Finally he began to get ready. He put on his best uniform. He was brushing his hair when Charlie Bowers came by. He had been allowed to come into Richmond on a short leave from the trenches. The undersized drummer boy sat on a box and watched him. "What's up, Jeff?"

"Oh, birthday party."

"Whose birthday?" Charlie asked.

"Mine."

"Why, you son of a gun! You didn't tell me that. I didn't get you no present."

"You don't have to do that, Charlie."

"You'll be eighteen. Bein' eighteen, that's almost a man. I'd guess it makes you feel that way. Does it?"

Jeff remembered how badly he had been behaving. "Nope, not really, Charlie. I feel just like I did yesterday. Like I got a ways to go before I grow up."

"I remember the last birthday party I had at home. Sure was a good one. We had ice cream and cake and fireworks. Of course, it was the Fourth of July, so we would have had that anyway." Charlie leaned back, reminiscing. "It's too bad your ma didn't live to see you grow up to be a man. I bet she would've liked that."

"I expect she would," Jeff said shortly.

"My ma died when I was just seven," Charlie said. He polished his boot with the heel of one hand and looked up again. "But Pa married again two years later. I didn't think I'd like her after Ma, but I sure did learn to. She took care of me through all kinds of sicknesses. Pretty soon I loved her as much as I did my real ma. I just call her Ma now. Not that I've forgotten my real ma," he said. "But you know, I think she would have liked it, knowin' that her boy had a woman to take care of him. Don't you think so, Jeff?"

Jeff's throat suddenly felt very thick, and he could not speak. Finally he cleared it and said, "I guess you're right, Charlie."

Jeff soon left with Tom, but the words of the small drummer boy kept going through his mind. He could not get them out.

The front room at Uncle Silas's had been decorated as well as it could be under wartime conditions. Little cloth streamers hung from the chandelier. The instant he stepped inside, he was grasped by Esther, who began squealing, "Happy birthday! Happy birthday!"

Jeff picked her up and said to Leah, who was right behind her, "You didn't have to do all this."

"But it's my birthday too. Have you forgotten?"

Jeff said, "Happy birthday, Leah. I'm sorry I didn't get you a present. There's not much to be had in Richmond."

"I've still got this, Jeff." Leah fingered the locket that she wore around her neck. She opened it, and he looked at the old picture of himself. "You're going to have to have a nice new one made," she said. "You look much different now."

At that moment, his father's voice came from somewhere in the house. "Is that you, Jeff? Get on back here!"

Jeff, carrying Esther, walked quickly down the hall, followed by Tom and Leah. When he entered the dining room, he saw a white cake with lighted candles on the table.

"Make a wish, Jeff." His father grinned. He was not wearing a nightshirt this time, and when Jeff looked at him questioningly, he explained. "I couldn't stand not having my pants on anymore."

"I'm glad to see you're better, Pa."

"I'm on the mend. Now, you and Leah get over there and blow those candles out. I'm ready to start eating that cake. It smelled so good, I've been chewing my lip all day."

Jeff stood on one side of the table and watched Leah cross to the other side. They leaned over the cake, and he whispered, "Esther, you blow the candles out."

"All right."

"Ready?" Jeff said, and when Leah nodded, they all blew together, Esther blowing as hard as either of them. All the candles went out.

"Happy birthday, Jeff."

"Happy birthday, Leah."

Then Jeff saw Eileen standing at the door, wearing a light blue dress and looking very pretty. He knew that, whatever he did, he would have to do quickly or he would lose his nerve. Still holding Esther, he walked over to her and said, "Mrs. Fremont, I've got to say something to you."

Eileen took a quick breath. She glanced at his father, then back to Jeff, and said quietly, "What is it, Jeff?"

Jeff let his eyes run around the room in desperation. He saw Tom staring, a frown on his face. Leah wore about the same expression. His father looked as worried as he had ever seen him look.

Jeff turned his eyes back to Eileen and took a deep breath. "Well, what I want to say is . . . you and Pa can get married if you want to. I'd like it real well."

Silence hung over the room, and then Tom slapped his hands together and exclaimed, "Why, you crazy coot! They don't need your permission!"

But Eileen reached out and took Jeff's hands, ignoring Tom. "Yes, I really *did* need for you to say that, Jeff. Thank you very much. I'm looking forward to our life together. I've always wanted a son, and now I've got two and a beautiful daughter as well. God has been very good to me, and I'll do the best I can for you and for your brother and for your sister and for your father."

"Well said!" Nelson cried. He was near enough to take Jeff by the belt and pull him closer. The wound in his side was still obviously touchy, for he winced, but he said, "I'm not able to get out of this chair, but I want to tell you that this is your mother, and if I ever hear of you givin' her any trouble, you know what to expect."

Jeff grinned down at him. "I know that all right, Pa. I'll do my best. I can't promise anything though. I get pretty rambunctious at times."

The colonel held out his free hand, and Eileen came to take it. When he had it fast, he looked up at her and said, "It's good to have a wife and mother again."

After the cake had been eaten, and the small presents—all handmade and very inexpensive—had been given to the two honorees, everyone played games in the parlor for a while. Then Eileen went to the piano, and they sang old songs.

But finally she said, "Nelson, you're getting tired. We're going to put you to bed."

Jeff immediately got up, saying, "That's right, Ma. Make him mind." He discovered it felt good to have someone he could call Ma.

When Tom had gone back to camp and Esther was asleep, Leah sat with Jeff on the front porch.

"That was one of the hardest things I ever did— tellin' Eileen I was wrong," he said.

"You always did have trouble doing that. But so do I," Leah said. "I guess we're too much alike."

They watched the huge moon. It was almost orange and seemed pasted on a black-velvet sky.

Jeff said quietly, "I've never seen a moon brighter than that."

"It is pretty, isn't it?"

Quiet fell over the porch. Far off a dog barked, and then the bark turned into a mournful howl. The shadow of an owl drifted across the front yard, and they both watched the bird glide away into the darkness.

Jeff said, "I'm going to be goin' into the regular army tomorrow."

"I wish you didn't have to do it, Jeff."

"I'm eighteen now, and that's a man of legal age. And I wouldn't be true to the Confederacy if I didn't."

He got to his feet restlessly. "Let's walk down the road a piece. It's almost bright as day."

"All right."

They strolled along the road in the moonlight, saying little, and when they reached the crossroads, Jeff said, "I guess we better go back." But he hesitated and then turned to her. "You're seventeen years old now."

"Yes." Leah looked up at him. She could remember when they were both the same height. She had been tall and lanky, and Jeff had gotten his growth slowly. Now, however, he was six feet, and she felt secret pleasure in looking up at him. She had always felt big and gawky, but now she did not feel so. "I'm seventeen," she said, "and that's a woman."

Suddenly Jeff reached out and grabbed her. "A woman?" he shouted. "Tomorrow I'll throw you in the river, just like I did when you were a little girl!"

"Jeff, turn me loose!" She laughed and tried to get free, but his strength was too great. Then she stopped struggling and just looked up at him.

"I remember a little girl I used to hunt birds' eggs with. She had braids, and big eyes, and she felt she was too tall and gawky. I wonder where that little girl is now?"

"And I wonder where the little boy is?" Leah said. She still made no attempt to pull away. "I guess they're gone forever, Jeff. But we can remember those days, can't we?" She took a quick breath, for he suddenly released her hands, put his arms around her, and pulled her close.

"I guess if you're a young woman, then you need a birthday kiss." He kissed her soundly, then grinned. "Well, I guess you're a woman after all."

Leah started back up the road, but he caught up with her and took her hand. They said little until they got within sight of the house.

Then she said, "Jeff, be careful when you go back to the lines. I couldn't stand it if anything happened to you."

Jeff squeezed her hand. "Don't worry. God's brought us too far to let anything happen to me now."

They turned into the yard. The dog on the porch thumped his tail and lifted his head to greet them. They stopped on the steps for a final look at each other.

Jeff said quietly, "Nope, you're not a little girl anymore, Leah Carter."